A Modern Lady

Denise Daye

DEDICATION

For my husband and son without whom this book would have been completed months ago.

Don't forget to sign up for our newsletter to get FREE romance novels. You can find the newsletter and more info about our books here:

Thank you!

TABLE OF CONTENTS

CHAPTER 1

*H*e was disgusting! Never before in her life had Isabella met more foul of a man. The burning in her eyes intensified as her stomach churned. She was sitting before her favorite opera—Mozart's *Magic Flute*, a piece that had always cheered her up, but not this time. No, not even the energetic, colorfully dressed bird-character Papageno had managed to lift her spirits. Isabella's gaze was directed downward, and she bit her lower lip so hard she could taste the metallic flavor of blood in her mouth.

"This is my favorite part," hummed the culprit of Isabella's agony into her ear, totally out of tune and ignorant to her suffering.

Unlike Isabella, whose golden hair, sky-blue eyes, and kind heart made her a beauty in every way possible, Lord Warrington, her betrothed, was old, overweight, had bad acne, and was constantly sweating, which led to him carrying soaked, smelly handkerchiefs in his pockets at all times. But that wasn't the reason for Isabella's disgust. Certainly

Warrington was by no means her first choice of marriage. If it had been up to her, which it hadn't, she would have chosen a man who was at least somewhat kind, or funny, or caring, or even just polite. If Lord Warrington had possessed even one of those traits, it could have made this godforsaken arranged marriage somewhat bearable. But Lord Warrington was none of that. In truth, as impossible as it might sound, he was uglier on the inside than he was on the outside. Renowned for his drinking and whoring problem, no respectable family of society would consider marrying their daughter to him, which was the very reason he was still unmarried at the age of sixty-five.

No family could bear the thought of placing a beloved child into the hands of a man who was known in all of London as "Sucking Willy," a nickname he received after rumors made their rounds that he liked to wear nappies and breastfeed when he made his nightly visits to the brothels. Who in their right mind would marry their daughter to such a man?

That was precisely the point that Isabella struggled to comprehend. *In her right mind* could by no means be used to describe her mother, Lady Astley, at this point any longer. Isabella caught a glimpse of her mother out of the corner of her eye.

She seemed so content and entertained by the opera despite her own daughter's misery; it felt surreal. Was this all a nightmare? Would she wake up at any moment now, before her awful engagement to the most insufferable man on this planet would be announced this very evening after the opera? But before she could let herself feel the slightest hope, she felt that sweaty hand on her knee again. It instantly tore her from her thoughts and back into the nightmare she had to call reality. *Pig!*

For the third time this evening, she moved her leg aside, out of reach of the very hand that left smelly sweat stains all over her dress. Isabella shuddered in disgust, grinding her teeth with a hatred and anger she had never felt before. As if Mozart himself had stepped out of the grave to comfort her, the Queen of the Night started singing the part of the opera that made the piece so famous and could have not been more fitting for this very moment:

> *"The vengeance of Hell boils in my heart,*
> *Death and despair flame about me!"*

It was right there and then, listening to those very words carried to her by the Queen of the Night—feeling Lord Warrington's wrinkly, sweaty palm creeping its way up her thigh to the part that no man should ever touch without a woman's consent, seeing her mother's happiness despite throwing her own daughter away like an old hat that had fallen out of fashion—it was right there and then that Isabella could take no more. Overtaken by emotions, Isabella whipped the back of her hand across Lord Warrington's face with a slap so powerful, it might very well have been the slap of the Almighty himself.

"Get your filthy hands off me!" she shouted like she had never shouted before.

The opera continued, the performers seemingly unaware of the events, but a few people—her mother and Lord Warrington included—turned in utter shock. Seeing her mother's wide stare, and realizing a moment too late what she'd done, Isabella jumped from her seat and fled the balcony in such terror one might think the devil was after her. Flying down the stairs, she didn't slow down until she heard the large, golden entrance doors of what was once her favorite place slam behind her. The unforgiving cold air of a crystal-clear night slapped Isabella's face as she stood, frozen in shock.

"How dare you!" a sharp voice hissed from behind.

Isabella didn't have to turn around to know who it was.

"How dare I? How dare *I*? Surely you're not serious!" Isabella spun around to face her mother, causing a few of her golden locks to come loose from her bun. Her blue eyes glittered with anger, like those of a cornered animal ready to fight for its life.

"Oh, I am entirely serious. You are acting like a spoiled little brat." Her mother frowned arrogantly, unemotional, the same flat tone Isabella had had to endure all her life.

"No Mother, I am acting like any normal woman would considering the circumstances," she shouted back at her in despair.

A couple walked by, speeding up their pace, pretending they'd heard nothing to avoid embarrassment. Isabella's mother burst into high-pitched, fake laughter, pretending nothing was the matter.

"My dear child you are too funny." Lady Astley laughed loud enough for the couple to hear.

But as they faded into the distance, her mother's face burned into an uncontrollable rage. She clenched her fist around Isabella's arm and dragged her forcefully into the side street next to the opera.

"You listen to me, you ungrateful wench. This marriage is not ideal but it is necessary. Lord Warrington is the fifth richest lord in all of England. I would have preferred a marriage to the Blackwells, but unfortunately for us the old Blackwell kicked the bucket before Lady Blackwell and I could seal the deal between you and her son, who now shows as little interest in marriage as you do… So that is that."

Isabella drew her brows together in anger. "I thank God for that! William Blackwell would have been just as awful as your current Prince Charming. Why were none of the other men acceptable to you? Age and looks aren't important to me, but some of them were at least kind, like Father."

Isabella jerked her arm in an attempt to free herself from her mother's painful grip, but without success. In response she clenched her fist even tighter.

"Don't be ridiculous. They were just as useless as your *failure* of a father who left us with nothing to live on. We would have run out of their money in no time."

Her blood ran cold. Isabella knew that her mother spoke the truth. Not the condescending remarks about her father, a gentle, kind soul who had passed away from a weak heart about two years before. No, she was right on target about *her* money problems. Her mother had single-handedly managed to put her father into the ground by spending his fortune—riches that had been in his family for hundreds of years—at a speed he was unable to recoup. After years of working himself to death, his heart finally gave out, and he'd died from the stress of being married to a woman Isabella had to call mother. That was the beginning of the end of one of England's finest houses, now on the brink of ruin.

In a last desperate attempt to save Isabella from the despicable marriage their mother had arranged for her, George, her kind-hearted brother, had journeyed to America in the hopes of making a fortune. But time was running out, and their self-absorbed mother had decided that it was time to fill her depleted chests with gold by marrying her daughter off to a rich monster. But unlikely as it was for a lady to defy her mother, Isabella too had made her decision.

"Well too bad, Mother. Because I would rather live in the poorhouse than marry that creature." She pointed toward the Opera House before raising a hand into the sky. "And by God, I swear I mean it!"

For a moment they both stared at each other, eyes filled with hate. One stared in disgust while the other watched in pity. It was the Duchess of Aberdeen who broke the silence, exploding into loud, unladylike laughter, swinging her hand fan wildly in front of Isabella's face.

"Child, really. You should have been born on a theater stage!" Her laughter sounded like a cat being strangled; she was laughing so hard that it brought tears to her eyes. "For a moment I almost believed you, child!" Her elegant chest chuckled up and down. Unable to contain herself, she finally let go of Isabella's arm, leaving visible red marks.

Isabella tucked her wrist into her other hand to ease the burn on her gentle skin. Her gaze followed her mother's finger wiping away a tear of laughter out of her pretty eyes. Back in the day, the Duchess of Aberdeen had been an exceptional beauty—the very reason why her father, the widely respected Duke of Aberdeen, had married her in the first place. It was a mistake he had come to regret for the rest of his miserable life, which had ended not too long ago. And now, thanks to her greedy mother, her father's misery seemed to have turned into a curse that would haunt an entire generation of Astleys to come. No, she wouldn't allow it. Isabella would stand her ground.

Unfazed by her mother's conduct, she decided it was time to speak from the heart.

"If you really want to save yourself from ruin, dear Mother, then I suggest you marry Lord Warrington yourself."

Without the slightest interest in witnessing her mother's reaction to those words, Isabella turned and walked away. Experience had taught her that there was no point arguing any longer when her mother reached this point of anger. She would not marry this man, no matter the consequences. She would just have to stay for a few months at her aunt's home. Her father's sister, who happened to hate her mother even more than Isabella did right now, would certainly take her in until society moved on to the next subject of gossip. But before she was able to reach the other side of the street, her body was pulled violently as she was forced to turn around. Once again, she was under her mother's deathly grip, mother and daughter eye to eye as they both stood still in the middle of the road.

"Do you really think I would marry a pig like that?" Her mother's eyes burned like the hellfire that she most likely ascended from when she came into this world. Her nostrils throbbed as though red-hot steam was fuming out of them.

"Mark my words, you ungrateful brat. If it's the last thing you'll do, you will marry Lord

Warrington and save me from ruin," Lady Astley growled, eyes narrowed.

Was that a threat? Isabella thought. A threat to do what? Her mother was shaking, brows tightly drawn together in rage. Isabella had experienced her mother's anger before so many times she thought she had seen it all. But this was different, in a terrifying and almost vile way. She glanced over at the woman in front of her that she called mother. For a moment she was unsure who she was, and what she was truly capable of. How much further was she willing to go? How desperate could she possibly be? After this engagement, she had thought nothing would ever surprise her about her mother. But was she mistaken?

Isabella flinched and shut her eyes the instant she saw her mother raise a hand. It wouldn't be the first time she would endure violence from her own mother. But instead of a well expected slap, it was the cold sting of silver that hit her in the face, followed by a ringing from below as whatever her mother had just thrown at her face bounced on the hard pavement. As she opened her eyes, she noticed a spark of light that rested beside her feet. It was a single shilling. Her mother had just thrown a coin at her face, hard enough to hurt her, most likely even to leave another mark.

"If you don't marry Lord Warrington, I swear to God, or the devil himself, or whatever creature is listening, that this is all you will be worth after I have finished with you."

Those were the last words her mother spoke before leaving her in the middle of the street, alone in the bitter cold that had started to assault her fair skin, along with nothing more but the very coin she'd priced her at. Isabella felt empty. She felt lost and sick to the core. She tried to blink her tears away, but her eyes were focused on the silver beneath her. A shilling. That's what she was worth to her mother. A shilling. Nothing more, nothing less. Out of all the babies born every day, why her? Why did she have to be born an Astley? How she wished for a different life, far away from here. What would she give if she could just disappear, to a different place, to a different life, to be someone else. Anybody else. Poor, ugly, short, boring... None of it mattered as long as it was far, far away from here.

The street was as dead as she felt inside. Maybe she should just give up. Marry Lord Warrington. Get it over with. At least her brother's estate would be saved. He was as innocent in all of this as she was and didn't deserve to die in poverty because their mother had wasted away his inheritance. Isabella bent over to grab the shilling, ready to give up all hope of love, or of being loved.

"OUT OF THE WAAAAAAAAY!"

Her ears were hit with a loud scream, followed by the sound of screeching wheels and thunderous hooves, before she was flung into the air so hard she felt her spine snap in two. Her body slammed onto the ground so fast that there was no time to scream in pain. Her eyes flickered. Her vision phased in and out. A glimpse of bright light in the distance — then everything went dark.

In her mind, Isabella knew exactly what had gone on. A carriage must have hit her. Was she dead? Just like that? One moment still breathing, one step closer to freedom, then the next dead in the ground? Well, at least she would not have to marry Lord Warrington any longer. Not the kind of escape she had in mind, but if that's what destiny had in store for her, she would have to accept it nevertheless. In her last moments of consciousness, her final thoughts were dedicated to her brother, for whom she wished all the love and happiness in the world.

CHAPTER 2

Isabella squinted from the harsh lights of the carriage beam in front of her. She must not have been out for as long she thought; after gaining consciousness, for a brief moment she even doubted the idea that she had come back into this world again.

"I… I am still alive." Her eyes flickered as she whispered under weighted breath. "I thought I was dead."

"Thank God I was able to hit the brakes in time." A pleasant male voice spoke gently. "You have no idea how relieved I am."

Kneeling next to her, a tall figure was partially blocking the blaring lights. It took her a moment to realize that this tall figure was actually holding her torso in his arms while her legs crumpled on the stone-cold pavement. Her eyes tried to open all the way, but this carriage had the most incredibly bright lanterns she had ever came across. She flinched. *What sort of candle was this? Or is it some new type of gas lantern perhaps?* She held her hand up to her face, blocking the lantern that had seemed to turn night into day, catching a glimpse of the tall figure who held her. He must have been in his early thirties. His face was well defined with sharp lines and angular cheek bones. His hair was dark and full, with a few lightly curled strands falling onto his forehead. And although it was hard to make out any colors in this ridiculously bright lantern light, his eyes managed to glow out a warm, amber brown. His gaze locked onto her as she struggled to steal a breath. Gosh, he was attractive.

"How are you feeling? Are you hurt anywhere?" the man's beautiful voice asked, sounding as if he really cared.

"I'm fine." Her gaze fell to her hand, then traveled up her arm and to her shoulder and down the rest of her body. Odd, how fine she was considering the hurt she'd just been through. With the help of the carriage driver, she managed to pull herself back up on her feet, only to find herself frozen in place. She noticed that there were no horses attached to his strange looking and loudly humming carriage.

"Where are the horses? Did they run loose?" She spoke in a low voice that almost sounded like a whisper. The man tilted his head, staring at her like she'd just said something silly.

"Horses?"

"Yes, the carriage horses."

Isabella scouted out the street. Her eyes opened wide as her pupils reflected every light that shimmered around her. She was surrounded by oddly shaped metallic carriages that were a lot smaller than the ones she was used to. They all lined up quietly at the side of the street. Unlike the carriage of the man in front of her, none of them were humming a strange noise nor shining any lights.

"I-I don't understand. What is all of this?" she stuttered, throwing her arms up into the air. The man stepped closer, holding his hands in front of him in a calming gesture.

"This must be very scary for you. I was hit by a car myself not a long time ago. It would be better to get you to a hospital."

Did he say a car? Is that what this is called? Isabella's eyes narrowed as she caught a glimpse of the man's clothes. *What a strange suit. Is he a foreigner perhaps?* He wore some sort of blue pants and a white cotton shirt without buttons. It had a black checkmark sign on it, similar to the sign on his white shoes made out of some fabrics. A moment of thought hit her. This was clearly not the same place she had been hit by the carriage. Had this man moved her? Had she been abducted? She felt her heart racing under her chest.

"I… I don't understand what is going on! This doesn't look like London at all!" she yelled, her eyes glued to the man, demanding answers. But the man only stared at her with his narrowed eyes and lips slightly parted for a brief moment, enough for her to notice, before finally deciding to speak to her. "No, ma'am. We're in Philadelphia."

She was right. He was a foreigner. At least that explained the man's accent. Wait. The man's accent? Philadelphia?

Isabella threw her palms to her forehead hard enough that she almost slapped herself. She was clearly losing it.

"Philadelphia?" she whispered to herself but audible enough for the man to hear.

"Yes, we are in America, ma'am," the man said with a worried look on his face.

"Are you saying…this is America? Not England?" Her legs felt weak as she wobbled, nearly stumbling back to the ground as the man swooped in, holding her by the elbow. Under normal circumstances, she would not let any man, certainly not a stranger, hold her so close in such an unladylike manner. But Isabella was far too deep in thought to notice.

"I think we should really get you to a hospital." The man's voice snapped her back into reality. Embarrassed for being too close, she wanted to pull herself away — but she didn't.

The man pulled out a strange black device from his pocket that lit up like a star for a fleeting moment before turning pitch black once more. *Does everything turn bright in this country?*

"Damn it. My battery's done. I'll just have to drive you. The hospital isn't — "

"That won't be necessary." Another strangely dressed man with a much younger sounding voice stepped into the bright carriage light, appearing out of nowhere. He wore a black hood pulled far over his face as if he didn't want to be recognized. "I will take it from here," was all he said before he grabbed Isabella by her arm and pulled her away.

"Who are you?" she instantly protested. "Let go of me!" She tried to break free. There wasn't even time to put up a fight as the carriage driver placed a hand on the hooded man's shoulder, pulling him back.

"It doesn't look like she wants to come with you, pal. So why don't you get out of here before I have to make you?"

For a second, the hooded man seemed unsure what to do, but decided to make the wrong choice. He pulled at her again, tightening his grip as he tried to hasten his speed, dragging her behind. Isabella cried in pain which was enough to force the carriage driver into action. With a single punch, the hooded man fell to his knees, letting go of Isabella while he gasped for air.

"Let's get you out of here," the carriage driver said as he gently pulled her away from the strange assailant.

Isabella stopped, turned around, undecided what to do as she stared around her. She felt a gentle tug.

"You'll be safe with me," he said with a reassuring tone. She scanned him from head to toe. Maybe it was his pretty face, warm smile, or the fact that he had just saved her, but strangely enough, she believed him. And with that, Isabella made her decision to go with this man she had never met before.

He led her toward his metal carriage and opened the door from the side. How bizarre it was that she had to bend down to get in and sit down. Warm air blew from a vent in front of her while tiny lights sparkled around. Isabella was so fascinated with this carriage she didn't even notice when the carriage owner reached over to tie her down with a black, smooth rope. Before she could even resist, she realized how close his face was, and how much his scent had overtaken her, sweet yet strong with a hint of spice. Was he a prince or a lord? Or perhaps a man in power? Isabella knew that only men with a certain degree of status could be bothered to use such fragrances. But he was so different than all the other arrogant lords she had met before.

"We don't want you to get hurt again…or get me another ticket." He smiled as she noticed a dimple in his cheek. She had no idea what he was talking about, but it was obvious, at least to her, that he was a good man with good intentions. And before she could even ask how the little orchestra managed to play from out of the rectangular light filled with numbers on it right next to her, the man shifted a stick right below the little orchestra box, and the carriage started to move. With each second it became faster and faster. It made her heart race and jump as her stomach flipped. But the man, the carriage driver beside her, seemed so calm and unfazed that it made her feel embarrassed, so she tried, with a bit of effort, to hold down her nerves.

Remembering the man that had attacked her, she turned to look. To her surprise, the hooded man was on his feet again and started running after them as if he was trying to catch up with the strange carriage. But it didn't take long before he became smaller and smaller and finally disappeared in the distance. *Who was he? What could he want from me?* Her questions seemed to be written all over her face.

"Do you know this joke of a man?" her savior asked in a tone that implied he was ready to turn around to give him more of a beating if she would like him to.

"No. I have no idea what is going on. Really. I don't understand any of this." She truly didn't. Had she gone mad perhaps? Died and gone to a different world? Heaven? Was America heaven? Or hell? "Well, whoever he is, he has some nerve to try to assault someone who just got hit by a car. Right in front of me too. Unbelievable!" He slapped his upper leg with one of his palms. "People really have lost all common sense." He shook his head in disbelief.

"Liam, by the way."

"Excuse me?"

"My name. I'm Liam." Americans seemed to use first names right away. She actually liked that. It seemed so much friendlier than all those stiff titles.

"Oh yes, of course. Isabella Astley."

"Were you on your way to some sort of costume party?"

Isabella followed his gaze over her dress. "Is my dress not according to the latest American fashion?"

"Emm… Well… Don't get me wrong. You look fantastic in it. But your dress looks like it's out of some nineteenth century period movie."

"Nineteenth century, what? Do you mean this is not 1881? What century is it now?"

Liam drew his brows together and stared at her with the exact same worried gaze he had earlier when she mentioned London and horses. "Twenty-first century…," he mumbled, seemingly concerned.

Did he just say twenty-first century? TWENTY-FIRST CENTURY? She wanted to laugh out loud, doubt him, but something was obviously going on here. Something incredibly extraordinary. She stared out the window. Wherever or whenever this was, it couldn't be more different from everything she knew. The houses were built high up, some of them high enough to touch the skies. And still not a single sign of a horse carriage on the streets. Everywhere she turned there were stores that flickered and glimmered, glowed and blinked in colorful lights. As insane as it sounded, her eyes confirmed what Liam had just told her. This could very well be the future. Or she'd hit her head hard enough that this was all a dream.

Liam glanced over to her. "Don't worry. I may not be a doctor, but I highly doubt that your head trauma will be permanent. I think I was able to brake before the car hit you too hard. I assume it's the shock, or maybe you hit your head tumbling backward? Whatever it is, I will make sure you get whatever you need. I will also provide the hospital with my information and insurance card. Or we could even call the police from there if you prefer that."

"The police?" A cold shiver ran down her spine. "Oh, please no!" What an awful thought. What if her mother had somehow traveled along into the future with her? Or worse, what if it was a head injury and she had lost her sanity for the time being? That would give her mother the power to put her into an insane asylum, or at least threaten her with it and use it to her advantage. No—no police. And no hospitals either. That would be better for her until she was able to find out what the bloody hell was going on here. Liam did the confused stare again. *You have to be wise now, Isabella!* She had to be more careful around people here so as not to raise their suspicion.

"I mean, that won't be necessary. As you say, I must have fallen or something. It's not your fault that I was standing in the middle of the road at a time any other respectable lady would be in bed…" She tried her best to give him a shimmering smile.

"Right. But…I am still responsible for all of this and will do whatever needs to be done to make it right. What were you doing out all alone? Did that man chase you or something?"

Telling him about her disagreement with her mother would complicate things. He might want to have her come to the hospital like any concerned mother should when her child was in need. But her mother was not like that. It was quite the opposite. It would equip her mother with the ultimate weapon against her.

"No. I have never met that man before. I was picking up a coin I dropped." She opened her hand for the first time since she'd bent over to grab the very shilling that was possibly the cause of all of this. She barely remembered picking it up, but for some reason knew all along that it was right there in her hand, subconsciously protecting it with a clenched fist like her life would depend on it. And in some ways, it might. She wasn't certain yet how, but this shilling played a role in all of it. It was a gut feeling, she just knew it. Liam took a quick glance at it before averting his gaze back to the road.

"What a strange-looking coin. What is it?"

Oh, Isabella you fool... If this really was the future, how wise would it be presenting items from the past? From now on it was best to pretend to be from this world. This accident had now turned into a blessing. At least she could blame a lot of her strange behavior on a head injury that she might or might not actually have in reality. Even she wasn't sure what was going on with her.

"It's...it's an antique coin from Europe. I collect them," she said with an unconvincing smile.

"That's a pretty unique hobby for a young woman."

"Young? Ha! I'm twenty-three!" she said, looking proud of herself as if she had the wisdom of the world under her belt. Liam grinned. Something she said must have amused him.

"We're here." The car came to a halt and Isabella looked out the window. Like everything else in this strange world, the hospital was built up high into the sky and was awfully bright as well. It had big, glowing letters written on top of it that said "UPENN." Liam was about to get out of the car, but Isabella grabbed his arm.

"No." For obvious reasons, he looked confused.

"I would rather go by myself if that's okay?"

He wrinkled his forehead at her.

"It's rather personal."

He seemed to be thinking about her words for a second.

"Of course. It's really up to you, but are you sure? I would feel a lot better if I could go with you. To make sure you're safe and that they have my contact details in case they have questions."

Isabella couldn't help but feel like for the first time ever, somebody besides her brother actually cared about her. Naturally that was not the case.

How could it be? This man barely knew her. But still, his kindness was something she had never experienced before. It warmed her heart and put a genuinely contented smile upon her lips. She straightened her back, taking a bold breath in to face him.

"Liam, please believe me when I tell you that I am extremely grateful for all you have done for me…"

"I almost ran you over with my car."

"Yes, but that wasn't your fault. I should not have been in the middle of the road in the dark. You saved me from that strange man, and you also drove me here. That is more than most people would have done. But I am in no need of further assistance from here in." Still gentle, her grip on his arm tightened a little, just enough to let him know she would not accept no for an answer. It was obvious that he didn't like any of this, but the gentleman that he was, he would accept her request. She knew it. He took a deep breath and forcefully blew out again. A sign that he accepted her wish, even if he didn't agree with it. He reached behind to get a black wool coat from his backseat.

"Fine, but take this. I won't have you freeze in the waiting room of this place. They can be quite cold and the doctors can take hours before they get to you. Believe me, I have been in them more times than I would like to admit."

It made her really uncomfortable, but she accepted it with a thankful nod. This could be necessary for survival out here in the cold. He opened the black strap that held her in place and put the coat around her shoulders. How kind he was. She couldn't help but stare at his pretty face. Suddenly, for some reason she didn't know, her gaze wandered to his lips. Even in the low light of the car she could see how soft and pretty they were. His face was so close now, if she leaned in just a little their lips would touch. A warm, wonderful tingle formed in her stomach. Isabella couldn't help but blush. What the bloody hell was going on with her? She had just traveled into a different world and would be left to fend for herself any second from now, but she had nothing better to do than be romantic?

For a second it seemed like he'd frozen in this position, just long enough to make her notice but not long enough to question his intent. She put her hand on the handle of the door next to her. She saw Liam use it before so it was quite obvious what it was for.

"Thank you. I really appreciate everything you've done. Besides my brother, who isn't really around anymore, nobody has ever been this nice to me. I will never forget your kindness." Isabella twisted her lip into a faint, gentle smile. For a moment it looked like he was about to say something, but then he shook his head in what looked like a combination of sadness, confusion, and disagreement over not going in with her.

"Here." He pulled a wallet out of his trousers and handed her a card from it. "My name, number, and address are on there. Please give this to the staff at the hospital to make a copy. And also the police in case you change your mind. I will of course cover all medical expenses and whatever you should ask for. In case you need anything, and by anything I mean *anything* – a ride, someone to listen, the moon – it doesn't matter. Please call me."

She held it in her hand for a moment before putting it into her coat pocket.

"I will." No, she wouldn't. This would be the last time she would ever see this man. For some reason it saddened her a little bit. "Thanks again." It took her two tries, but she managed to open the car door by herself and got out. As she stood in the middle of the night in a strange world in front of what Liam called a car, all alone, her strength almost left her. Doubt flooded her mind. How could she possibly pull this off? Walk out into this foreign country all by herself? According to others, not even a country of her own time...

She turned around. Liam had gotten out of the car and was leaning over its top, staring at her. If she didn't leave now, he would most likely change his mind and insist on coming with her. Then what? She would continue to say unusual things and he would grow more and more suspicious of her mental state, ultimately arranging for the doctors to admit her to an insane asylum.

How her heart gathered the strength to walk toward the entrance of the hospital she didn't know, but her feet carried her in that direction. For a brief moment she stopped in front of the glass doors, wondering where the handles were, but her question was answered as the door swung open by itself. She walked inside and noticed instantly how everybody stopped what they were doing for a moment to look at her. They must think her insane, dressed like this. She peeked over her shoulder. Liam was still standing there.

"May I help you?" a nurse asked Isabella, startling her as she did not expect her to be standing so close.

"Oh...no, thank you." The nurse analyzed her with a strange look from head to toe. That would not do. She had to try something more believable. "I am sorry, yes, you can help me. My friend…we were on our way to a costume party and she fell. I just wanted to see how she is doing, but maybe this is the wrong hospital?" Isabella looked over her shoulder again. Liam was still there. She admired his caring nature but right now it did not work in her favor.

"Was she dressed like you?"

"Y-yes. Dressed like me."

"Then I'm afraid this is the wrong hospital. Try Thomas Jefferson. It's right around the corner from here." The nurse leaned sideways to get a glimpse of the front door of the hospital. Liam was finally gone.

"Looks like your ride just left. Do you want me to call you a cab?" Isabella had no idea what a cab was, but she guessed it was best to say no.

"No thank you, that won't be necessary."

"Are you sure? This isn't the safest part of town. Especially not at night." Isabella had no idea where to go or what to do, but she knew she couldn't stay here, risking a straight ride into an asylum. All of this was still too unfamiliar for her to successfully pretend she was from this world. And who would believe her that she in fact was from 1881?

"Yes, he just parked around the corner. But thank you." And just like that, she stepped out into the cold dark night of an unknown world. All alone and frightened like she had never been before. What would she do now? She took a deep breath in, holding it for as long as she could.

"You wanted your freedom, now make the best of it," she told herself in a firm voice, trying to convince herself that this was nothing she couldn't handle. With those words on her mind, she stumbled into the dark and cold night of twenty-first century Philadelphia.

CHAPTER 3

A loud banging noise tore Isabella out of her sleep. It was bright out and the sun was shining, turning her struggles and fears from last night into a distant memory. She was cowering against the cold brick wall of a small alley, hiding behind a big green container that had the word "Dumpster" written on it. For hours she had walked the streets of Philadelphia last night looking for a church. They usually took care of the poor in her time, so she hoped the church's kindness extended into the twenty-first century. Unfortunately for her, the two churches that she stumbled across were both locked. It was in front of a church called "His Mercy" that she noticed a man following her. She didn't get a close enough look to confirm if it was the same man who had attacked her earlier, but whoever it was, she doubted that he only wanted to share a lovely cup of tea with her.

Isabella did the only thing that in that very moment made sense—she ran. As it turned out, her sixth sense did not fail her, as the man started to match her pace. Her heart beat wildly against her chest as she pulled up her dress and ran as fast she could. It was absolutely terrifying. She ran for her life, which wasn't easy with high heels while dragging a heavily decorated train behind her. This guy, whoever it was, had all the advantage in the world over her and should have caught her to do God knows what with her. But ironically enough, the very train in the back of her dress that made the escape so difficult in the first place ultimately saved her. She had just turned into an unknown side street, unsure about how much longer she had it in her to keep running like this, when her legs tripped over the train and landed her flat on the pavement. Hidden behind the cars, she heard the man's footsteps pass by her on the opposite side of the street. For how much longer she decided to stay there on the ground, afraid to even breathe, she didn't know, but it was not until she heard the loud bark of an angry dog that she jolted back up on her feet. She rushed into an alley and hid behind the same dumpster that now had awoken her.

Isabella got up to stretch herself. She was hurt from the fall last night, skin bruised and clothes tattered, but she had no choice but to keep pushing forward into this strange, new world. She scouted out the alley, but nobody was there. Whoever had slammed the lid of the dumpster was now gone. Her white gloves and light pink dress were covered in dirt. Slowly, she stepped out of the alley and into the same street that had made her heart race and burn just a few hours ago. But unlike last night, there was light, real light, as the warm sun made everything, for a moment, seem cheerful.

Fascinated by everybody and everything, Isabella surveyed the street. Everyone was dressed in male clothes, even the women. They were going about their business, riding bikes, walking their dogs. Was that a woman walking out of a bank? Were women allowed to have their own bank accounts here? It immediately stood out how much more independent women seemed to be in the twenty-first century. They were walking by themselves, without maids or a governess. It was almost as if women here were free to do what they pleased without others questioning their reputation. Isabella stared at a young man who must have been her age walking by with white ropes hanging out of his ears. The man gave her a strange look as he passed by without turning his head. Cars just like Liam's were driving by, giving the whole scene a lively touch.

The sun felt incredibly good on her frozen face and she closed her eyes as if last night was just a bad dream and she was just another twenty-first century woman. How exciting this world was!

Wandering through the streets last night, she had seen the strangest, most intriguing things. Pictures in windows that were constantly moving, showing images as if they were real. She heard music out of apartment windows, like everybody had their own orchestra. Wherever she ended up being, the wonders around her seemed endless.

"Look." She heard a little boy laugh and point at her. The boy's mother pulled him to the side and scolded him for making fun of her. She then gave a warm smile at Isabella, her way of apology.

"Kids can be cruel little bastards, you know," a rough voice coughed from behind her. Isabella instantly turned around to find that it belonged to an old woman dressed in rags with thin, nonwoven bags hanging around her wrists. She had white shoulder-length hair and looked like she had been through a lot.

"But at least you know where you're at, if you know what I mean," the woman continued. Whoever that woman was, she must have been homeless.

"I never looked at it that way, but I agree." Isabella couldn't help but dedicate her reply to the very symbol of deception—her mother.

The lady came closer. "Sorry for waking you earlier. I try to get to these dumpsters early before the others make their rounds. There hasn't been a single morning that I didn't find something useful in them. Especially this green one—never disappoints if you know what I mean…"

The woman looked back and forth in between the dumpster and Isabella, establishing a silent connection between them. That was definitely a hint that Isabella shouldn't ignore. She knew exactly what this woman was talking about—her, she talked about finding her. From now on she needed to attract less attention. Isabella looked down at herself. This dress was a magnet for trouble. She needed to find clothes that didn't make her stand out like a flamingo in a flock of pigeons. Now, not later.

"That is good to hear. I wish you best of luck then. Will you excuse me?" Isabella walked down the street but noticed the homeless lady following her out of the corner of her eye.

"I didn't mean to scare you," she wailed from behind.

"You didn't." Isabella didn't stop.

The woman kept following her, squeezing in a few lengthy steps until she was walking right next to her.

"You look hungry." She smiled wide enough to show a broken tooth. What was it with these people in twenty-first century not minding their own business?

"I am fine, thank you." Isabella tried to pick up speed.

"Where are you from? Not from here, are you?"

"No, I am from...somewhere far away. Will you excuse me now?"

Isabella turned into a side street and looked over her shoulder to catch a glimpse from behind. The woman stopped following her.

"Okay, but you look like a flamingo in a flock of pigeons."

Isabella came to an abrupt halt. Was she a mind reader? The cold reality of her situation hit her. This wasn't a bad dream. She was trapped in some sort of other world, or time. Whatever was going on here, Isabella needed to get out of these clothes and find shelter. The thought of another night like the one she had just survived sent shivers down her spine. She had learned the hard way this was, in fact, more than she could handle—without help at least.

"There is no shame in accepting help, you know. And you look like you need plenty of that," the old woman continued.

Isabella turned around. The woman had raised some valid concerns. Up until last night, Isabella didn't even have to tie her own shoes. What made her think that she was weathered enough to survive this alone? In a different country...CENTURY! *Asking for help is a sign of strength.* Her father's words repeated in her thoughts. He never lived by his own advice, which was the reason for his tragic downfall. No, she wouldn't follow him down that path. This lady was right. She needed plenty of help.

Isabella heard her stomach growl so loudly she wondered if the old lady had heard it.

"I was just on my way to get some breakfast at the church. You are welcome to join me." The woman pointed behind her down the street. Isabella took a good look at the woman from head to toe. Just like with Liam, none of her protective senses seemed to go off.

"To be honest, I did find myself in a rather peculiar situation and wouldn't mind some food and fresh clothes."

"There you go." The woman looked proud, as if she'd just returned a lost sheep to its shepherd. Why was she helping her?

"Just follow old Dan," the woman said, turning around.

"Dan?"

"That's me. Dan."

So women here had male names. Why not.

"Isabella."

The woman started walking toward the direction of the green dumpster again. "Well, if you don't mind, I will finish my rounds on the way to the Church."

"Of course." Isabella wasn't sure what Dan was talking about but at this point it didn't matter. She was willing to do whatever was required of her if that meant that she could get some food and could finally get into fresh, twenty-first century appropriate clothes.

"Next time we shall clarify 'rounds,'" Isabella said, out of breath, as she pushed her shoulder into Dan's butt so she could reach into what she swore to be the last dumpster.

"Just a bit more. I almost got it…" Dan huffed back, out of breath.

"There it is!" Without warning she pushed herself back out of the dumpster, causing Isabella to tumble backwards onto her butt.

"Will you look at this? One woman's trash is another woman's gold."

With a big grin, Dan held up a pair of broken glasses. She put them on and locked her gaze onto Isabella.

"I knew you were a lady, but I had no idea how pretty you were."

Dan walked right in front of her and stretched her hand out. But just when Isabella reached for her hand to help her back up on her feet, Dan bent over right next to her, picking up a quarter while Isabella lost her balance again, landing on the same spot with her butt on the floor for the second time since she'd met Dan.

"Will you look at that," Dan said in an excited voice, holding the quarter into the air.

Isabella let out an exasperated sigh. This woman was not easy to be around. However, she had taken the time to run after her and offer her help. It wouldn't be right to complain about anything at this point.

"What are you doing there on the floor? Didn't you say you were hungry?"

"No, not at all, Dan." She got back up and brushed the dirt off her filthy dress that less than twenty-four hours ago was the latest Victorian fashion.

"Well let's make another round east then. The dumpsters there —"

"No! Please! I was being sarcastic. I am starving."

"Oooooh, sarcasm, I see. How unusual for a lady. But I guess those times are behind you now." There it was again. Dan mentioned the word lady. Strangely enough she talked as if she knew who Isabella was. But that was impossible, of course.

"I know you're hungry but it might be wise to get you some clothes first. You're a bit out of fashion, I'm afraid."

"That would be very kind if you could help with that."

"No worries. You're with Dan now. Well, don't just stand there. There's a store right around this corner."

Dan led Isabella to a small clothing store that was, as she said, around the corner. The freedom women had in the twenty-first century to choose their own fashion was something Isabella had admired since last night when she'd passed by several shop windows. Women were dressed comfortably like men, in pants and shirts showing arms and legs. How simple it must be to put these clothes on. A stark contrast to what she'd had to go through every single day in 1881. Dressing was no easy task for a Victorian lady. First there was the uncomfortable, fluffy underwear, followed by the squeezing-all-air-out corset, followed by the corset outerwear, followed by the actual dress, topped with countless accessories. Without those, a proper woman was not considered dressed.

Like a Christmas tree, servants would put on gloves, hat, undersleeves, ruffles, a shawl, parasol and fan. One simply didn't just pull up pants and put on a shirt and be considered dressed. And what for? All that effort just so that men had something nice to look at to make themselves feel fuzzy on the inside…exactly like a Christmas tree. Hours every day wasted simply because men wanted it that way.

A feeling of joy overcame Isabella when they entered the store and she picked up a pair of jeans as if it was the most normal thing to do.

"Are you certain this is deemed acceptable to wear? I can put this on all by myself!" Isabella giggled like a child in a candy store. The owner of the shop, a young woman wearing too much makeup, now stepped closer, analyzing first Isabella and then Dan with an arrogant look.

"This is not a charity place. Get out before you make things dirty!" She scowled.

"Don't wet your panties, we have money to pay," Dan growled.

The shop owner mumbled something to herself but didn't interfere any further. Isabella, flabbergasted, felt a pang of guilt as she stared at Dan's money.

"Gosh, Dan, I am so sorry. How childish I must seem to you, coming here without money."

Naive and childish indeed. Of course, she needed money to purchase clothes. Although she had never paid in person before—her servants would do that—she wasn't from the moon either and knew that things weren't free. Embarrassed, she quickly put the pants back.

"I don't have any money." She looked down onto the floor.

"Of course not," Dan said with a calming gesture, waving her hands. Was it her looks? The fact that she slept next to a dumpster? How did she know?

"I cannot take that from you, Dan."

And she couldn't. Dan was poor, homeless, and had to go through rubbish to make ends meet. How could she take that money from her?

"I won't take no for an answer, child." Her tone was unyielding. "I have nothing else to spend it on but cat food anyway. And those stray little bastards will be fine for a few days. They are way tougher than all of us street folks combined."

She nodded her head. Isabella was moved. To everyone, this woman was nothing more than some homeless person dressed in rags. But to Isabella, she was one of the kindest people she had ever met and wondered how her life would have been if her mother was, at least the slightest bit, like Dan. Who else would give away money in her situation? She hated the fact that she would have to accept Dan's offer without giving something in return. So, she took off her earrings and necklace. Not the finest pieces she possessed but real pearls nonetheless. "Here. I shall trade you instead."

Dan shook her head. "That is too much. I won't have none of that nonsense." She waved her frail hands.

"Well, we have to leave then, and I shall stay in my filthy, wet, cold, and thanks to you, now also rubbish-stained dress." Isabella grinned, knowing she had just won the argument, but Dan needed another little push.

"Just keep it safe for me until I can repay you, please." Isabella handed her the earrings.

"The cats. Until you can repay the cats," Dan corrected her.

"Yes of course," Isabella agreed, handing her jewelry to Dan who this time accepted it with a growl.

"Blackmail," Dan mumbled to herself.

The shop owner peeked over a rack of clothes, carefully watching their every move with eagle eyes. Isabella started browsing the shop, picking up a few things that were the least expensive.

The store had some sort of buy-one-get-one-free promotion as they called it, so she ended up with two pairs of jeans, two black wool sweaters, and a pair of some sort of running shoes. She didn't need a coat as she still had Liam's, and although it was way too big, it was warm. It didn't matter to her right now what she would look like. Surviving was more important. Isabella stopped in front of the shop's mirror on her way out to get a closer look at her outfit. It was amazing. She looked just like all the other women passing by on the streets now. Her whole life she had been raised only to wear the finest clothes and was expected to look down on others. To have servants pamper her like an infant, regardless of her age, but not anymore. No. She was her own woman now. A woman wearing jeans and wool sweaters and running shoes. A free woman with a life in America. And although her life here had seemed hopeless hours ago, thanks to Dan she now had a chance at it.

The church Dan was taking Isabella to was just a few streets away. Now that it was later in the morning, the streets were buzzing with life and the walkways were littered with people who flooded the streets, coming from every corner. Cars were honking, dogs were barking, and buskers were playing music entertaining those who walked by. The twenty-first century was as overwhelming to Isabella as it was stunning. She could barely walk straight as her body shifted from left to right, taking in every little view that the city had to offer as she stopped here and there and pointed at things with her mouth and eyes wide open in disbelief. A young man stopped next to them at the light that would tell you to stop or cross the street. He had one of his feet on some sort of rolling cart that had handles. Isabella was in such awe, she grabbed it by the handle and turned to Dan with a big smile.

"It's a rolling foot cart!" she blabbered. The young man threw her an angry look.

"It's a scooter," Dan said patiently while pulling her hand back off its handle.

"Crackhead," the young man hissed, rolling his eyes, and rolled off as fast as he could as soon as the light turned green.

"I'm a crackhead!" Isabella said smiling at Dan as if it was the biggest compliment in the world.

"No...you ain't no crackhead." Dan dragged her across the street before the light turned red again.

"Come on now, I'll explain things to you on our way." Dan obviously seemed to have noticed how much Isabella struggled to take everything in and decided to speed things up by dragging her and commenting on the people who walked by as if she was trying to help her understand this world from scratch.

"Businessman," Dan said when a man in a modern version of a day suit walked by.

"Student with a backpack," she continued. "Old woman dragging a dolly with groceries. Another student holding a device called a cell phone. Friends going for coffee..."

Dan went on and on, commenting on almost every single person who passed by. Isabella nodded in total awe at everything and everyone. Suddenly, she stopped as she noticed a big rectangular box mounted to a wall behind in one of the shop windows. It had music coming out of it and looked like a reflection of the real world. Like a child, Isabella pressed her nose against the window, staring at the box with a huge smile and sparkling eyes.

"Dan! Look! Over here! This box is playing photographs in color!" she shouted, barely able to control herself. Dan walked a few steps back to join her.

"That's called a TV. The photographs you see are real." Isabella was about to ask how this was even possible when she realized how strange she must seem. Like an insane person, ready to be locked away in an asylum. She took a few steps back from the window and stared at the floor.

"What is it?" Dan asked.

"Don't you think me strange?" Her voice was so low, it almost sounded like a whisper. How could she not? Isabella was acting like a little child. Everything was new to her. That would have been understandable if people knew that she had time-traveled here from the past. But that was part of the problem—nobody knew that!

"No, not necessarily," Dan said, placing a hand on her shoulder. "You know, there was this guy at the Church who talks to bedbugs." Dan shook her head, thinking back. "Now that's what I find strange. But you?" She stared at her with her wrinkly face and cracked glasses. "You not so much."

Isabella was not convinced. Why was Dan helping her? Being kind to her? She had to make things look as normal as she could, even in front of Dan who seemingly accepted her for who she was. "I suffered from a head injury. It makes me forget things," Isabella said, trying to make an excuse for her odd behavior.

Dan grimaced as if she did not buy that at all. "That's a good idea. Let's tell other people that so they don't think you're psychotic." Dan nodded in approval over her idea.

"Psychotic?" Isabella asked. She'd never heard of the word before.

Dan grabbed her arm and gently pulled her down the street again. She leaned close to her ear. "You know. Crazy... Talking to plants, hearing voices, dancing naked around trees. Those type of things."

Isabella crossed her arms. "Well, I am certainly not psychotic."

Dan took a deep breath, shaking her head in a mix of annoyance and sympathy.

"I know that. But others might not." She grabbed Isabella's arm again and said in a soft, caring tone, "Come on now. I'm hungry. We will figure things out down the road."

Isabella's stomach growled like a tiger's roar. "Yes, I am rather hungry myself."

She took a good look at Dan's face for a brief moment. Her instincts told her that she was no threat and only wanted to help. It reminded her of the carriage driver last night and how, deeply worried, he'd held her in his arms. She wondered where he must have been by now, and when she realized that her mind had wandered in thought, she shook her head to jolt herself back into the present.

"I didn't mean to be harsh. Thank you for helping me."

"Let's go then," Dan said. "I'm getting hangry."

With a heart so filled with emotions it was ready to burst, Isabella followed Dan down the street into a new chapter of her twenty-first century life as a free woman.

CHAPTER 4

It was late. Isabella closed the tent's zipper behind her as she fell onto her improvised bed made out of clothes and newspapers. She stayed with Dan in her two-person camping tent in an alley behind the police station. Quite a genius move on Dan's end. Nobody bothered her here. The police had come to know Dan over the years and they even protected her little tent once when city authorities tried to remove it.

Rolling over onto her belly, she turned on the little radio Dan found about two weeks ago. Both of them loved listening to it until they fell asleep. "White noise," Dan called it. Listening to classical music, Isabella reflected on her new life in America and everything that had happened up until now. Those were by far the most bizarre, unthinkable, far-fetched and, at the same time, most incredible weeks of her life. Nothing came even close to it.

As insane as she might sound, she absolutely loved it. Here she was, Isabella Astley, daughter of one of the oldest and most respected houses in all of England, living the life of an American twenty-first century homeless person. The thought was so preposterous, she couldn't help but burst into laughter wondering what her mother's reaction would be if she could see her right now. It gave her a great deal of satisfaction that she was still alive and free, even though it was far from what anyone in 1881 would call thriving. At least she had her freedom, something she and many other women didn't have in 1881.

"Screw you, Warrington," she whispered, rolling onto her stomach. Screw was one of the words Dan had taught her to sound more American.

Sure, she had fallen low, from gold linens to dumpster newspapers. But as Dan always said as she stared at the sky from a small hole in the tent, only people from way up there can feel the loss of falling all the way down here. If you're already living down here, you'll barely notice a thing. Isabella unwillingly had to agree with that.

Every day, Isabella would aid Dan in her early morning dumpster runs, which always ended in feeding a horde of feral cats at a park close by. In return, Dan would teach her about the wonders of the twenty-first century. Some made sense, others were too complex for her to understand. But all caught her mind in awe.

To this day, Isabella wasn't sure why Dan was helping her and how much Dan really knew about who she was. Lucky for Isabella but unfortunate for the rest, people didn't pay attention to the homeless. They were generally considered insane by society in the twenty-first century, which sadly had not changed from her own times. It never seemed strange to anybody that Isabella had no idea about even the most basic things of this world. And in the rare event somebody did wonder, Isabella just said that she'd had a head injury, a perfectly plausible excuse. Dan knew that this wasn't the truth, but she never asked questions.

Over the past three weeks, Isabella had learned about the most astonishing inventions: cell phones, computers, airplanes, movies, and even how to search what Dan called the internet, a library of everything that exists, accessible on those devices called cells and computers. Not that Isabella could afford one of those magical machines, but Trent, an old social worker at the church where they ate lunch and took showers, was kind enough to let Isabella play with his phone while he volunteered at the soup kitchen.

As marvelous and magical as everything in the twenty-first century was, her favorite item turned out to be a small black box called a radio. For hours she would sit next to it in Dan's small tent as they both listened to various stations, trading thoughts and sharing laughter. And from these moments, for a single brief moment, she would see her poor brother sitting next to her. Overnight, he had left everything he knew and held dear in an attempt to defy their mother and save her from that awful marriage. Back then, every day she received a letter from him, telling her not give up hope, that he would try harder, that America was promising. If it wasn't for those letters, she would have not been able to keep on like she did. Until that eventful night changed everything.

She felt a pang of guilt that drove away the joy in her heart. She was living her freedom while her brother must be looking for her, sick to his stomach, not resting until she was found. Which in this case would be when? How? No, this new world, America, as much as she had come to love it, she couldn't stay. She would have to find a way home to him.

But Dan was always speaking of the future, telling her she would soon be able to start going to school, get an apartment, and that all she needed was a bit more time to "recover" from her accident. And then she would send her off into the real America, an America waiting to be conquered by a strong, kindhearted, beautiful English lady named Isabella. Yes, those were Dan's exact words. Little did she know that this would not be Isabella's future at all. Soon she would have to start working on her plan to get back into her own time. Back to the past. Back to 1881. Back to everything she hated, and to the few that she cared about. And like every night, just before she was about to sink into a deep despair, Jerry, an older and overweight police officer who worked at the station this alley belonged to shouted.

"Isabella! Turn that damn music off before people start calling me again with complaints!"

She sent him a faint smile into the darkness and, like every night, didn't turn it off but just lowered the volume.

"Flatfoot," Dan growled at Jerry, rolling over to her side. She didn't mean it in a bad way. Isabella knew by now that he was Dan's friend. One of the very few she still had.

Jerry was a good guy. He was not like the other "pigs," which was American for a mutton shunter, who treated the homeless like they were worth less than the rubbish they had to survive on. He checked in with Isabella whenever he saw her, always wondering what a pleasant young girl like her was doing living on the streets, which of course she never answered truthfully.

Isabella looked over to the silhouette of her dear friend. Dan was already sound asleep. She covered her with a blanket, twisting her mouth in disbelief about how much she had come to like this old, stubborn but selfless woman. She had become so much more to her than just a helping hand. She was almost like a mother to her, or at least what she thought a real mother would have been.

Like every night, half asleep, Dan checked under her pillow to make sure that the knife was still there. As much as Isabella enjoyed her freedom, being homeless was still a dangerous and cruel existence. Most of the people she encountered when out and about with Dan were not homeless by choice. Just like in her own time, they were outcasts, desperate lost souls forgotten and banned from society. For these people, life on the streets meant life or death. If it wasn't for Dan, Isabella had no idea where she would be now. Perhaps dead, and that was by no means an exaggeration. Dan had told her that folks had started to notice a strange man dressed in black and lingering in the shadows along the neighborhood each night for the past few weeks. By the morning, he would disappear and never be seen until the darkness once again enveloped the city.

Could this possibly be the same man from before when she first arrived? It was a strange coincidence that this man seemed to be found mostly in the street where Isabella turned up. All thoughts set her thinking about her mother. Had he been sent by her? Revenge for leaving her high and dry without marrying her beloved golden chest? The thought of it made her swallow an angry lump in her throat, making her sleep even more uneasy. Isabella pulled the wool coat up to her shoulders and put her head to rest on a self-made pillow.

Every night when her eyes closed, and her mind slowly drowned in a lake of dark thoughts, a soft light would glow. A memory of the man who held her close against his chest when she first came into this strange world. Liam. She'd remembered his face and his warm comforting smile. She had only met Liam once and barely knew him. Putting it off as childish thoughts, she turned to her side, trying to think of something else. But he always seemed to be the last thing on her mind before drifting off to sleep. Childish or not. Night after night.

Isabella woke up to the feeling of a cold hand pressed onto her mouth. The tent was pitch black. Unable to scream, she frantically wrestled the hand away in a sudden burst of terror as her eyes finally adjusted to dark. It was Dan, holding her mouth shut while placing a finger to her lips. Dan was holding the knife in her hand. She pointed at the tent's zipper, that was slowly moving upwards. Someone else was there opening it. Her blood ran cold. The pounding in her chest was deafening. Her hands staggered to find something she could use as a weapon. Anything would be better than her bare hands.

The zipper slowly opened, revealing more and more of a dark silhouette. Isabella was holding her breath in fear for what could have been the devil himself that now stood in front of them. All of a sudden, Dan threw herself screaming onto the intruder, like a tiger fighting for its prey. Isabella jumped out after her, fingers clenched against the small beloved radio box that she had now turned into a weapon. It was hard to see in the dark, but it looked like Dan was on top of a huge dark shadow. Her mind now made up to fight to the bitter end, Isabella threw the radio as hard as she could. The radio bounced off the dark figure's head, which was followed by a loud, male cry. The man countered by throwing Dan off him like she was a feather.

"Jerry!" Isabella squealed as she dived down toward the ground to reach for the knife that Dan must have dropped somehow. The intruder forcefully kicked the knife away.

"Jerry!" Dan yelled as she struggled to get back up. Out of nowhere, the blue lights of a police car started flashing up and down the alley. For a moment, the intruder stood looking at Isabella as if he were debating if all of this was worth fighting a cop over. He must have decided that it wasn't, as he jerked around and ran off into the night, disappearing in the dark like the shadow of a daemon. And just like in one of those amazing moving photographs that Isabella had seen before and now knew were called movies, Jerry jumped into the alley with his gun pulled.

"Is everything okay here?!" Jerry rushed over right past them to take a quick look behind the tent before putting his gun away. He tried to help Dan back up on her feet, but Dan shook him off in pride, standing up by herself.

"No. That devil was here. Tried to snatch Isabella." Dan spat on the floor.

"For Christ' sakes, Dan, speak English!" Jerry shook his head, slightly annoyed. It was obvious that his nightshift had been a rough one.

"We were attacked by the man that people keep seeing lingering around the neighborhood." Isabella tried to break the tension.

"He tried to enter our tent. I... I think he might be after me for some reason," Isabella clarified. For the first time she noticed that her hands were trembling. Jerry noticed it as well. He leaned his head to the side, talking into the police radio on his shoulder.

"Two-J-two Dispatch."

"Two-J-two go ahead," a woman talked back to him over the radio.

"Show me code six. I have possible twenty-seven. Suspect fled northbound. Male, unknown age, dressed in all black. Possibly armed. Most likely Ghost."

"Roger that," the voice replied through his radio.

"Ghost?" Isabella asked, confused.

"Yeah. That guy. People who can't be found in the system. No records. No matches. Nothing."

Jerry sighed frustratingly. "We're already looking for this guy. I have been trying to chase him down a few times after receiving scared calls from neighbors who said he was standing out front on Fifth Street. But he gets away every single time. So far he has been peaceful."

Jerry's gaze held Isabella's eyes. "But that seemed to have changed."

"Fifth? That's the street he attacked Isabella on after that car hit her," Dan said moving her wrist left and right to see if it was broken. Jerry instantly took the bait.

"What car hit whom?" he asked in a suspicious police voice. This conversation was heading into dangerous territory for Isabella. She stepped in.

"It was nothing, just a scare," she said hastily before Dan could give away anything else about the matter. Dan got the hint. But so did Jerry.

"Nothing, huh?" He shook his head in frustration. "Well, whatever nothing is going on here, it has to stop, Isabella. This is the end of your little runaway chapter. No offense Dan, but it's time we find Isabella's relatives and let them know that she's here."

Dan was outraged. "She is safe with me." She scowled, her hair still frizzled from the match, which made her look like a wildling. An angry one at that. Jerry wasn't fazed at all.

"Yes, I can see that…," he countered calmly but with a hint of sarcasm. That was more than Dan could handle. When it came to her beloved Isabella, she turned from a woman who didn't care about anyone or anything to a lioness ready to pounce.

"How dare you? I would give my life for this girl!" She shook her fist in a gesture that said all too clearly what she thought of Jerry's remark. Taking a deep breath, he changed his tone.

"I know, Dan, I know. But how is this supposed to go on? Living in a tent? Chased by a potential psychopath? Don't you want to see her safe—er? Safer?"

Dan didn't answer that but turned her head away from him. Isabella now stepped in. She wasn't that helpless lady from 1881 anymore and now had a say in what she wanted in life. She wouldn't let Jerry take her away from Dan.

"Thanks, Jerry. I know you mean well, but I will stay here with Dan. I couldn't possibly leave now. What if he comes back? Dan needs me."

Surprised by her own bravery, she crossed her arms to signal that she was serious about this. Jerry stared at both of them, wondering how to approach this situation the right way. He scratched his head but suddenly lifted his chin as if he'd found the answer to this problem.

"That's exactly the point. Do you really want to drag Dan into this? What if she gets hurt trying to defend you? And you..." He turned to Dan. "Wouldn't it break your heart if something happened to Isabella? You can't be with her every second of the day. God knows what could have happened if my shift would have ended an hour earlier this morning."

Neither Dan nor Isabella knew how to counter this. That was a genius strike on Jerry's part — making both of them feel guilty if something should happen to the other one. For a moment, the three of them just stood there is silence.

"He's right, kid." Dan was the first to speak. Under different circumstances she would have protested, told Dan that it was her choice where and with whom she frequented, but Jerry had raised a valid point. This man was after Isabella, and now she had managed to drag Dan, an older woman, into this. She had to disappear for a while. Away from these streets. But what was she supposed to do? Somehow Jerry read her mind.

"Don't you have family you can go back to?" A lie crept its way into her mind. But she knew it would only make things worse.

"No." She spoke softly.

"What about friends?"

Isabella shook her head.

"Otherwise I have to arrange temporary housing at a halfway house for you."

"No way!" Dan shouted at him, shaking her fist. "I won't let you put her in one of those holes, Jerry! They're full of drug addicts and you know that." Dan must have hit the nail on the head as Jerry didn't disagree but scratched his head as if he was searching for another solution.

"Is there really nobody else we could call? Even if it's just for a few days, it would give me some time to try to catch this guy."

Isabella hesitated. There was one person. But it would be quite unseemly.

"Maybe, but it wouldn't be proper…"

"Proper?" Jerry stumbled in shock. "Who cares about proper. Your life might be in danger."

Isabella had to agree with that. She nodded.

Dan stared at her in anticipation like she was about to announce the meaning of life itself.

"Who is it?" Dan and Jerry asked at the same time.

Nobody less than the man who seemed to be constantly on her mind.

"Damn it." Liam coughed, swinging the windows wide open to let out some of the smoke. The fire alarm was unbearably loud, hurting his ears like someone was slapping them. He grabbed a towel and swung it in circular motions above his head to clear the air. But the alarm didn't stop so he decided to just pull the batteries out.

Rambo, his incredibly chubby and strong-willed cat, thanked him for this move by poking his head out from the closet again. It was pretty much the only hiding spot left for him as Liam's apartment was almost completely empty. Besides a mattress in his bedroom and a table with two chairs, there was absolutely nothing left in it. No rugs, no pictures, no decorations...nothing. It was a small one-bedroom apartment in the shadier side of the University District. Quite the downgrade from his downtown five-bedroom loft. But it was all he could afford at the moment—and even that was barely manageable.

"I know, buddy, I know." Liam comforted Rambo for the second time before rushing back to his phone. He had been cooking eggs when the phone rang. Determined to tell whoever it was that he would have to call back, his whole plan was completely thrown off when he found out the police were on the other end of the line. He was so perplexed, he completely forgot about his breakfast on the stove.

"Hello?"

"Yes," Jerry answered, quite annoyed for being on hold for so long.

"Sorry about that, I thought my apartment was about to burn down," Liam countered, a bit annoyed himself. "So if I understand this right, you need me to come down to the station to get her?"

"Pretty much. She said you are the only person she knows."

How bizarre the whole thing was. Liam was just about to put that strange and peculiar encounter with Isabella out of his mind, but now the police were asking for his help. He tried to make sense of it all, but it only left him even more confused. The night he met her, he was driving home from another depressive night shift trying to save his company. His mind had been drifting into endless thoughts about his company and all the people who depended on it and before he could even blink, he saw a woman bent over in the middle of the road. He kicked the brakes with all the force his leg had to offer, coming into a hard stop strong enough that it would have pulled him out of his seat if it wasn't for the seatbelt. The car slid across the pavement and managed to stop just in time.

He could swear he didn't hit her that hard, if at all, but when he jumped out of the car to check, she was unconscious on the ground. In a freaking period dress! No, not one of these cheap online Halloween dresses. That thing was legit. The real deal. Never in his life had he ever seen one of those things except in the movies. As if that wasn't bizarre enough, Isabella was talking about horses, and carriages, and lanterns like everything around her wasn't meanderingly normal at all. Nothing would have been strange about this if he wasn't certain that he barely hit her. If so, then how did she get that head injury? But then, what's certain these days? If he was being honest, he couldn't even remember what he had for lunch yesterday. Trying to keep his struggling business afloat was more than enough stress to make him question his judgement.

"Is there a problem? Don't you know her?" Yes, Liam, is there a problem besides that you don't know her at all and that the police are asking you to pretty much hide her from a possible dangerous stalker? Every other man would have said no to the whole thing. Every other man would have told them that it would be better to not get entangled with the victim of a recent car accident who could potentially still file a lawsuit in court against him. He sighed, knowing the answer to such an unbelievable dilemma.

Liam was Liam, a man who not once but on several occasions had risked his own life to save a fellow soldier or pretty much anybody else who needed it during his five-year service in the military — and afterwards.

"No. There is no problem. I'll be there right away."

The officer hung up before saying another word. For a moment, he just stood there in silence, wondering what the hell he was thinking. But then, Isabella's sad words came back to him repeatedly, more than he liked to admit throughout the past few weeks.

"Thank you. I really appreciate everything you've done. Besides my brother, who isn't really around anymore, nobody has ever been this nice to me. I'll never forget your kindness."

Those were her exact words. Coming from a victim he had just hit with his car, most likely causing a head injury that made her think she was from a time when horses still pulled carriages. She should have been angry, threatened him with the police, a lawsuit, anything... But to thank him for driving her to a hospital stating it was the nicest thing somebody had ever done for her was one of the saddest things he had ever heard. What kind of a man would he be to not do whatever he could to help? There was a chance that he was the cause of her confusion. At that moment, he was aware of every beat of his heart. It felt like he was sinking. He knew the feeling... It was guilt.

"It's just for an hour or two. I don't want you to fall out of the open window." Rambo instantly protested with a heartbreaking meow from the other side of the door like the poor cat was being tortured. He loved sleeping on the mattress, but like every other cat, only on his terms — not with a door closed by a human.

For a moment Liam considered changing from his jogging pants and sweatshirt into one of his nicer outfits. He shook his head, surprised by the fact that he'd even considered it. It was seven in the morning and he was on the way to the police, not a romantic dinner date. He grabbed his keys amidst the smoke that still floated in the air and left his empty apartment as the door closed behind him.

CHAPTER 5

L iam was impressed for a moment by how much those police stations looked like they did in the movies. The room he entered was stuffed with messy desks that had tired-looking officers sitting at them, typing away on old computers. It wasn't hard to spot her. Isabella sat next to the desk of an older cop who Liam guessed must be Jerry, the officer who called. She wore a pullover wrapped around her shoulders. For a while, Liam stood there, stealing glances, until her bright blue eyes finally noticed him, piercing through him like a knife against butter.

How did he not notice her beauty before? But then, looks were not something he usually paid attention to any more. Those days of checking out women were long gone, or as his older sister always said, he'd matured into a real man who understood true beauty. Or so he thought he did, until he saw her again.

She smiled at him, catching him off guard. Feeling embarrassed for whatever reason, he instinctively smiled back, which was more of a grin. Jerry on the other hand did not give him a warm welcome. His eagle eyes analyzed him from head to toe. Liam cautiously walked right next to Isabella.

"You ready?" he said as if they'd known each other for years.

"Yes, thank you," she replied in a soft voice that clearly signaled appreciation. Liam reached for the big plastic bag right next to her, and sure enough it had her crazy huge period dress in it partly poking out. There were some other items in it which he did not want to bother looking at for being called a creep.

"Is that all?" He couldn't help but be a bit surprised by how little she possessed.

"Yes, I'm afraid so," she answered, her cheeks turning red in embarrassment.

"We'll get you whatever else you need, I promise."

She didn't answer him and turned to Jerry as she stood ready to head out.

"Thanks for everything, Jerry," she said to the man on the desk who, in turn, had his gaze still locked on Liam.

"I will check in on you and Dan as soon as I can," Isabella stated as if that was a sure thing.

"That won't be necessary." Jerry got out of his chair.

"I'm sure Logan here —"

"Liam," he asserted.

"Yes, Liam. I'm sure Liam here won't mind me checking in on you. It's better if you stay away for a bit until this guy is caught... Or would that be a bother for you, Liam?" Jerry squinted at him, adjusting his gun belt.

"Not at all."

"Daily," Jerry added.

"As many times as you'd like," Liam repeated, unfazed by him. Isabella and Liam were about to make their way out, passing by the clacking sounds of officers typing away on their keyboards, when Jerry's voice broke through the noise.

"You served?"

Some of the officers stopped and looked at Liam. He wasn't surprised by this question. He already expected that Jerry must have run his name through his computer before calling him.

"I did." His voice was steady as it echoed across the momentary silence.

Jerry nodded in respect. "Thank you for your service."

Liam nodded back across the room of officers who now stared at him before making his way with Isabella out into the bright sunny day.

Isabella had checked her reflection in the mirror of Liam's car more than once now. For the first time in three weeks she cared about how she looked. Her heart was softly palpitating under her bosom. She could never forget his face since the night she met him, but now she was able to study his incredibly easy-to-look-at features for the first time in broad daylight. He looked nothing short of irresistible. His black hair perfectly matched his sparkly but kind brown eyes. He had a body built like that of an athlete. He was tall and muscular but lean at the same time. His skin had a natural darker complexion like he'd just spent yesterday sunbathing on the beach. It was flawless. He turned his gaze, and their eyes met in the side mirror where she stole long secret glances as she clumsily looked away. She felt the sides of her face grow warm.

"Is there anything you could think of that we should get before going back to my apartment?" Liam broke the silence.

"N-no, thank you. I have all I need."

Liam glanced over at her plastic bag on the backseat. "Are you sure?"

"Yes."

"I'm afraid you are way too humble. No woman that pretty should have to manage with so few things. I kind of want to insist on taking you on a shopping spree." He grinned.

The word *humble* caught her attention. Never had she been called humble before, and for good reason. She was part of what people here in America would call the top one of the one percent. Not too long ago she was no better than those arrogant folks who turned their backs on the homeless. Living with Dan for the past few weeks had taught her a lot about life itself. But above all else, it had taught her humility. Never before had anybody looked down on her like people did when she was on the streets. In her time, nobody would ever have dared. Not a day went by when Isabella wasn't bowed to by servants. Looking back at it now, she felt a touch of shame about herself. How ignorant she was, ignoring the poor in their employ the way she did. If the twenty-first century had taught her one lesson that she would treasure for the rest of her life, it was that humans should be equal, and that where you are born is simply a matter of luck, not privilege as she had been taught all her life.

"That is too kind of you, but I must beg to differ. I have a bit of money and would like to reimburse you for any expense this short stay might impose on you."

Liam drew his brows. Darn it. She was talking too politely again. Like a duke's daughter, which she was, but not here.

"I will pay you back for food and I don't need anything else, thank you." That was better.

"There's no need for that. Once we file an insurance claim, you'll be surprised how much money you're entitled to." He grinned at her.

She didn't answer. She knew she couldn't file any claims as she wasn't even documented in this country. Besides, she wouldn't do it anyway. None of this was Liam's fault and him helping yet again without hesitation clearly showed what a good person he was. If only her mother had engaged her to a man even just a hundredth of the man Liam was, she wouldn't even be here right now. Better to change the topic as Liam seemed too eager to file that claim for her or take her shopping.

"So, you're in the military?"

"Was. Not too long ago."

"That's very honorable."

"I guess that depends on who you ask, but yes, I tried serving my country."

"Tried?" Her brows perked up.

"Once you see the horrors of war... you start to question what it's all for." A moment of silence loomed in the air amidst the endless sea of cars and people across the road.

"I guess that makes sense. Though I think it's still honorable of you to have done so. It takes courage to do that."

"Courage. Desperation. I guess they're both the same in my case."

Isabella stared at him, even more curious of the man who now sat next to her. "How so?"

"I was young and poor and it was pretty much the only way out of my old run-down hometown before I would end up getting into too much trouble." He smiled, seemingly in a trance like he was staring back into memories which only he could see. "But I'm glad I did it. I met people who I now consider my brothers and sisters. Women and men that would not hesitate to give their lives to fight for freedom, to fight for those in need. I don't have much family besides my sister, you know, so those friends mean a lot to me."

No family... Fighting for freedom... Those were things Isabella could empathize with more than he knew. "I know what that feels like. Not having anybody."

"So you really are all alone here?" His voice softened, and he took a quick glance before focusing back on the road.

"Pretty much." She stared out the window, leaning her head on the car seat with her fingers tangled with each other. "I have Dan, but that's it."

"Is Dan that lady Jerry was talking about?"

"Yes."

"Well, she sounds like a good friend."

"She is... She is with a friend until things are safer."

Liam gave a sidelong glance.

"Hope you don't mind me asking, but how did you get here? You sound like you're—" He hesitated for a moment. "From somewhere else?"

Isabella looked away, lips pressed together as she shrugged her doubts away. "I am. But I don't remember how I got here, or what I'm doing here. Everything before the accident is blurry."

That was a bunch of nonsense and they both knew it, but Liam didn't ask anything further. It was Isabella's turn to bring up an uncomfortable topic.

"Liam, I'm not sure how much Jerry told you about my situation, but someone odd has been stalking me, like a shadow—always there."

"I know. Jerry told me. You think it's the same guy that grabbed you when we met?"

"I'm not entirely certain," she said, thumbing her fingers, "but I do believe so."

"Don't worry. I promise you, if this psycho comes anywhere near you, I'll finish what I started that night. He won't be able to hurt anyone, or you, anymore."

There was no need to explain why those words felt so true. Liam was an honorable soldier. The mysterious man was no pushover, Isabella was sure of that since the encounter, but Liam was no rookie. He had fought for his country, for his life, and for others; besides, she saw him fight that night.

"Do you have any idea why he's after you?"

"No." Slightly, she bit her cheek. That was kind of the truth, but in the farthest corner of her mind, she pictured her mother. She might have had something to do with this. In the end, she had no clear clue what was going on here. She had no choice but to let things unfold on their own.

"Or he might just be a pervert. A pretty girl like you is just their type. There are so many stalkers these days, it's pretty crazy." This was the second time he called her pretty. Her cheeks flushed as her thoughts scattered into unfamiliar places. She never cared much for looks anyway. Thanks to her shallow mother, she knew that beauty, more often than not, was nothing but a shiny apple that's rotten on the inside.

Liam pulled in front of a townhouse that seemed to have been transformed into several flats. It had a cute porch in front of it. The whole street was lined with trees. For someone who had just spent weeks on the streets, it looked marvelously enchanting.

"How charming!" Her eyes were elated.

"Wait until you see the inside." He laughed out loud. She didn't understand what was so funny until Liam opened the door to his flat. It was empty. Almost completely empty. The flat had no entrance hall and led straight into the living room and open kitchen area. There was literally nothing but a table with two chairs inside it. Even the kitchen was totally empty. From the movies Dan had shown her, Isabella knew by now that this was sort of unusual.

"What happened?" she asked carefully, trying not to be nosy. Liam closed the kitchen window and walked over to a door that most likely led to the bedroom.

"A man," he replied with a big, sarcastic grin on his face.

"I know what that is like. Although my misery includes a woman as well," Isabella countered empathetically, suddenly realizing that this could be interpreted incorrectly.

"Not in that way," she said, backtracking her words. "The woman I mean. Not in that way."

Liam laughed as he opened the bedroom door. "Hey, I'm not judging. Love is love."

"Yeah, but in my case there was no love." Isabella turned away as her gaze fell on the bedroom door. "And that woman was my mother."

Liam stopped laughing, twisting pursed lips. "Sorry to hear that."

"She's out of the picture now," she said with a sad smile that wavered. "What about your mother, are you two close?"

The bedroom door opened a bit more and a tubby white cat came rushing out of the bedroom, rubbing against Liam's legs. He leaned over to pet the cat. She had never seen an animal be so close to a man. It wasn't considered manly in her time, especially not to cats. Men at that time bred horses for sport and luxury, not for pets. What a rare find of a man.

"I don't remember her. My father and mother immigrated here from Portugal with my sister before I was born. Sadly, my mother passed away of cancer six months after I was born." Liam slowly stood up as the cat continued to fawn over him. "My father missed her so dearly that he died of a broken heart two years after."

And she'd just said this stupid thing about her mother. Isabella's throat ran dry, staring at him with eyes wide open. How foolish of her. "I, I'm so sorry... I didn't mean to — "

"It's all good. My sister and I came to live with it. Plus, we were lucky to get adopted by a very nice farmer family." Rambo now tiptoed his way toward Isabella, sniffing the fabric of her jeans. Seemingly satisfied, the tiny critter began rubbing himself against her leg. She bent over to pick him up and scratched the little fur-ball under his chin. Rambo purred away like cat concert. It took a while for Isabella to notice Liam's face, staring at her with his lips slightly parted.

"What's wrong?" Isabella asked.

Liam shook his head in disbelief. "Impressive. Usually he's a jerk to everyone but me. Even my sister still gets hit by the world-famous and feared Rambo paw. She calls him the cat from hell."

Isabella threw her head back in laughter. Liam followed suit, and soon enough they both shared in an endless contagious laughter. She hadn't laughed this hard in forever.

"You must feel pity for me. I mean look at me," she said to Rambo, nodding toward the direction of her plastic bag sitting in the corner of the empty room. Liam stepped right in front of her to pet Rambo as well. His lips slowly turned into a smile.

"That's probably why he likes me too. I mean, look at this place, it's pathetic."

Liam opened his arms wide as if he was just presenting evidence to court. Both of them laughed out loud again, forgetting all their worries for a short moment, for the first time in months.

CHAPTER 6

Liam sat behind his desk staring out from his high-rise office window down onto the busy afternoon street. From the tenth floor, the cars and people down below looked like a big ant colony cheerfully moving across the modern jungle. A stark contrast from the bleak and somber mood of the office. The modern glass walls and freshly minted wood floors now seemed fake. His company used to be incredibly successful, bustling with people even though it had been founded less than three years ago.

It started out with nothing more than two eager young guys wanting a better life. One of them was Liam, the other his best friend Mike. Within a year, their little, unknown textile distribution company became a nationwide competitor in the world of textiles. The concept was simple but quite genius. Liam and Mike would travel all over the US trying to find small cotton farmers that were willing to start following practices necessary to get their cotton US Organic certified. A niche that was almost nonexistent. When Liam set out with nothing more than determination and a list with a bunch of names on it, he had no idea what he would find.

Much to his surprise, the vast majority of small farmers were barely getting by, always one step away from bankruptcy. They were thrilled when he presented them with a new business model, staring at him like he was some sort of gift sent from the heavens to save them. Within months, Liam was able to approach major US manufacturers with millions of bales of certified US Organic cotton at reasonable prices, right at the time of a huge scandal of harmful toxins found in baby clothing.

The stars had aligned and manufacturers were fighting over his cotton, begging to be moved higher on the company's waiting list. The two-man business exploded to a full-size company with over fifty employees. Liam's business model was not only pioneering but also fair to the farmers and his employees. Farmers were able to keep most of the profits for themselves. Liam never believed in bleeding them dry to make millions for himself or wasting money appointing overpriced CEOs. He then implemented a salary structure that would pay everybody the same, him included. What sounded crazy to most people was a no-brainer for him. Every employee, no matter what they were doing, was getting the same amount of money. This equipped him with a highly motivated and loyal workforce. The front desk staff made the same as the managers. Work-related drama was brought to zero, and people genuinely got along while staying professional at the business. Productivity and sales skyrocketed. Sick days were almost nonexistent. At the end of the year, everybody walked home with a bonus of the year's profits, which usually amounted to no less than $200,000. The company was featured in magazines around the globe. Thousands of resumes flooded them monthly, begging for employment at Green Wear LLC. Liam and Mike both came out as millionaires. So, what happened to the American Dream?

Like in so many tales of riches and power, the answer was greed. When Liam told Isabella that a man was the reason for his terrible financial situation, every word of it was true.

He'd known Mike since high school and they had been best friends ever since. They lost contact for a few years when Liam joined the military, but as soon as he got out, they were best friends again like nothing had ever happened. Mike moved to Philly to start the company with Liam. If only Mike had been satisfied with the three million dollars he made from the company in those three years, the

American dream would still be alive. Not just for Liam, but the rest of their employees along with the farmers.

But Mike wasn't. Without telling Liam, Mike sold his fifty percent share of the company to a big corporation that now wanted to change things around, turning Green Wear LLC from an employee-farmer paradise into a predatory cotton mill institution from the 1920s.

The bonuses were wiped out, minimum wage was introduced, the healthcare was terrible, and the farmers' profit were cut to keep them just one step away from bankruptcy again. Liam fought them tooth and nail, got the best lawyer he could, but the end result was the same. Owning half the company with endless capital in their pockets, they vetoed every decision essential to make even the smallest sales. Their plan was to dry Liam out financially to force him to sell his share. Undeterred, Liam used up every dime he had, taking out loans until the banks would lend him no more, all while he kept paying his employees and farmers for as long as he could. He was hopeful that the court would pick up the case soon enough to settle in his favor, as according to Mike's and Liam's founding contract, Mike was obliged to offer his share at a fair market value to Liam first before he would be able to sell it out. Of course, he hadn't done that and had sold his shares in secret, and now the new owner of these shares said that they'd bought these shares in good faith, which they didn't, and that their purchase was legal. Mike was nowhere to be found, missing one court hearing after another.

So here Liam was, broke, contemplating every decision that weighed on his shoulders, reading file after file again trying to solve what seemed like an impossible equation, when a voice jolted him out from his own head.

"Go home, Liam."

He heard the sad voice of his secretary Linda. She was an older woman whose fair share of tribulations was written all over her face. And unless a miracle fell from the sky, this would just be another glimpse of a better life taken away from her. Liam felt horrible about that.

"Not yet, Linda. Did the lawyer still not call back?"

Linda twisted her lips to a frown and shook her head. "No. But I told him earlier that he could reach you on your cell, so there's no need to sit around here any longer."

She was right. Liam got up and grabbed his coat. "If I leave now, do you promise you'll go home as well? There's really nothing else for you to do here either. You should stay home just like the others."

At some point Liam had given people time off. Why make them wait at the office day in day out when they could be with their families and save on daycare costs? If—and it looked more and more like it—Liam was unable to turn this around, they'd all lose their jobs overnight. This would be the last month he was able to pay for their salaries and benefits. All his own money was spent and the loans the bank was willing to lend him would be depleted of every penny, and nobody would see a cent. For some folks that wasn't the end of the world. They could find new work rather quickly, but for people like Linda, at her age, they'd be hard-pressed to find a job. And for the farmers, it could mean the end and closing down family farms.

"I hate making promises I can't keep. I like coming here. It gets me out of that empty house." Linda gave a frail smile.

Liam nodded in empathy. He knew the truth. Her husband had passed away several years ago. And her kids? They were selfish little pricks who only called her when they needed money. She had nobody but a tubby cat. Kind of like him, which was probably why he liked Linda so much.

"Go home, Liam. Now." Her eyebrows perked up in a commanding way. "I'll be fine here. I'm tougher than I look."

She gently pushed him away from his desk, nudging him closer toward the door. "And besides, don't you have a little lady friend at your house now?" Linda crossed her arms with a big grin.

"Whoa. Let me stop you right there. It's not what you think." Liam raised both hands.

"Mm-hmm…" She raised an eyebrow.

"Gosh, I should have lied to you and never told you about her."

"Impossible. It's written all over you. That walking therapy commercial face of yours seems almost joyful at times again," she teased him, poking a finger at his arm.

Was that really true? The morning after he picked up Isabella and walked through the office doors, Linda jumped in with a loud "Who is she?"

To this day Liam didn't know what it was that caught Linda's eye and accused him of romance literally one day after Isabella had moved in. Which, by the way, was a whole different set of problems. But Linda was right, he should head back home to make sure Isabella was okay. Jerry drove by his place and checked in on her frequently, but Liam still preferred to get home before the bright, lively town of Philly transformed into the dark, abandoned streets of the night; prime time for stalkers like the mysterious man, Ghost, who till this day had yet to be caught.

They had been living together for a few days now. Things had been a bit awkward around the house. Weirdly enough, it wasn't due to the fact that two strangers had been thrown into a small desolate apartment that didn't even have a TV (he had sold that too). No, weirdly enough, they enjoyed each other's company, and even Rambo loved her. What made the whole situation awkward were Isabella's efforts to do everything she could to stay out of his way. After a long back and forth, she finally gave in and agreed to take the bedroom while Liam slept on a blow-up mattress in the living room. He refused to allow any guest to sleep on the floor, especially not one he had hit with a car just a few weeks ago. But ever since that arrangement was set in stone, she disappeared into that room never to be seen again.

The first day, he thought she was just resting her head for a bit. But after two hours turned to four, then to six, then finally to eight, he decided to knock. She had a bathroom attached to the bedroom so that was not the issue. But what about food? Water? Was she drinking tap water? What was she doing in that empty room? He was working on his computer when he decided that after eight hours, that was it.

He found her wide awake, looking out the window as if it was a tv. She apologized for hiding, said she didn't want to be in his way, but to be honest, he wanted her to be in his way, to talk to him, to trouble him with whatever it was on her mind, or whatever it was that worried her.

By now he knew about her living out of a tent behind the police station with her friend Dan. At first, he was a bit mad that she'd pretended to go to the hospital, only then to disappear into a life on the streets. But her excuse that she feared to be admitted to a mental institution was understandable enough, and he couldn't help but admire her strength, resilience, and her incredible talent for survival.

Soon enough, she began to open up. Never had he met a woman who was so easy to talk to. Even though her words were few and selective, there was something about her that seemed almost noble. The way she spoke, moved, and laughed was as if she'd been raised by royals. She could wear rags and still pass for a queen. To go through the streets of Philly without complaining, seeing herself as an equal with those cast aside by society, surviving a near-death experience—that was not a thing anybody else he knew could just pull off. And all of this in a foreign country. No, Isabella Astley was not like any other woman he had ever met. To him, she was special, different.

Liam's heart pounded faster as he pulled up in front of his apartment. His feet drummed against the floor as he staggered to open the door, anticipating the conversation. To see her smile that lit up his gloom-filled day. To share that sweet laughter once more. He just had to get her out of that damn room again.

Liam couldn't believe it. When he entered the apartment, he expected to find the usual empty space with Isabella locked behind closed doors. But that couldn't be further from the truth. It smelled like food as he heard dishes rattling from the kitchen.

"Perfect timing, it's ready" he heard Isabella call out from the kitchen. He walked over to the table. It was set up for dinner, but in an odd way. Two plates each with two large knives, three large forks, a small spoon, a smaller plate to the top left and a water glass set to the right. It looked like the setup of a five-star hotel dinner. Isabella rushed by to put some pasta on each plate.

"I hope it's okay that I prepared dinner. I wanted to make up to you one way or another. I hope you're hungry." Isabella smiled.

He was beyond speechless. He was so used to coming home to an empty apartment, so used to a lonely life without a female touch in it. Sure, he had dated before, and he was by no means one of those pathetic guys that were unable to hold a relationship, chasing women barely turning eighteen to make themselves feel young again. In fact, Isabella was the youngest woman he had ever spent time with outside of work. But when he was in the military, he was constantly on deployment and after he finally got out, he threw himself and every minute of his life into building up his company. He simply had no time for dating apps and romantic dinners. But maybe those were all excuses? To put it simply, he had never fallen in love.

His sister often told him about the love his father had for his mother. Because of that, Liam wouldn't settle for anything less than love, for the sake of his future wife as much as his own.

"Thank you for making dinner." He finally snapped out of it. "You really didn't have to," was the only thing he got out.

"Would you have preferred I didn't?" She froze with a pot in one hand and a scoop of pasta in the other, staring back at him like she'd done something wrong.

"No-no. Are you kidding me? I was about to take down the door to the bedroom to see more of you." He laughed awkwardly, realizing how creepy that sounded. Jesus Christ, where did his good sense of humor go? Was he nervous?

"That was a joke. A pathetic one." Placing a palm of his hand in front of her. "I wouldn't do that of course."

Isabella smiled to set him at ease.

Liam took his coat and shoes off and they both sat down at the table. She stared at him with eager eyes as Liam grabbed the fork, taking a glimpse of her with a smile before taking a bite of the pasta. He froze... By God—this was the absolute worst food he had ever tasted! A sharp tingle of cayenne pepper and tabasco overpowered his sense of taste. It felt like somebody had struck his tongue with a whip with nails attached to it. His eyes filled with tears as he noticed Isabella waiting with big deer eyes. *Get it together, bro, get it together. You survived war, swallow it, you will survive this!* Eyes twitching, he swallowed it down without chewing it. God, he could feel it slowly burning its way down his throat, leaving a fire trail into his stomach.

"It's…" Tears were running down his red face. He coughed and finally got out, "It's deli—cious"

He choked, grabbing the glass of water, chugging it down in one move as if it were a life-and-death situation—which it maybe was.

God help me! Help me, Lord! He took another big bite under the watchful, proud, and satisfied eyes of Isabella. "Thank you. This is the first meal I have ever prepared."

"You are—" *Cough.* "Kidding. I..." *Cough* "Would have never guessed." He gasped for air.

Satisfied, she now took a scoop of the pasta and was about to bite when Liam instantly held her hand. It was too late; the damage had been done, to herself, he might add. She coughed up a storm, struggling to swallow that little bit of hellfire she'd just placed in her mouth. Begging for air, she spat it back out into a napkin before she grew as silent as a graveyard. But before Liam could gather himself to make her feel better, all of the sudden, she burst into loud laughter. Liam wasn't sure if it was okay to join her as he didn't want to hurt her feelings, so he mentally prepared himself to eat the whole God damn plate, even if it was the last thing he would do. But when he looked back at Isabella, throwing her head back, slapping her leg in out-of-control laughter, he couldn't help but burst into laughter too.

"It's absolutely insufferable!" Isabella howled, grasping for air.

"I was worried it might kill me!" Liam slapped a hand on the table, trembling with laughter. It took both of them forever to calm down again.

"I can't believe you actually tried to eat this. I don't think there's a kinder soul out there than you, Liam." She chuckled, wiping a tear from her cheek.

"This would have made it on the news." He grinned back, holding his stomach from the pain of laughing so hard. "A veteran soldier of five years was found dead after eating a plate of homemade pasta. He survived war, but not this…"

Isabella giggled, grabbing both of their glasses to get some more water.

"I'll order us some pizza. How does that sound?"

"Like a better plan than the one I had," she said, controlling her laughter.

Liam got up and walked into the bedroom to grab his laptop. He usually left it for Isabella during the day when he had no work to do so that she had something to do besides staring out the window. Jerry still wouldn't let her leave the flat unless absolutely necessary, as the perv was still out there somewhere. And none of them were taking any chances.

Liam opened the laptop, ready to google the pizza delivery's number, when he was greeted by dozens of open search windows and tabs. Isabella must've not known how to close them. It was bizarre trying to teach her how to use the laptop. She had absolutely no clue. Even simply moving the cursor was a struggle, let alone using the keyboard itself. But somehow, she knew what Google was, so maybe she'd just never held a MacBook before and was a Windows kinda girl.

He closed the first page to see that there was another right behind it. And another, and another — it never stopped. After closing twenty or so, he changed strategy and opened the browsing history tab to delete all pages at once. Moving the cursor over the "clear all" command, his brows slowly furrowed as he noticed some of the search terms displayed in front of him. *Time travel, how to get back in time, lost in different century, magical coins, witches, spells, alien abduction...* It was endless. His heart plummeted and he felt a wave of panic and sadness overcome him. Isabella was acting so normally, he thought her head injury had been resolved by now. But it was more than obvious now that this clearly wasn't the case! Was it all an act? Did she still fear being admitted to a mental institution? Or seriously believe all of this?

Liam almost dropped the laptop. What had he done? All of this was his fault. He was the one who'd hit her with his car. What was he supposed to do now? He took another glimpse of the search history, hoping it was all a mistake, that somehow he'd misread it all. But the same words presented themselves in front of him again and again, no matter how often he read them.

Her search history also included a George Astley, Duke of Aberdeen, and an address of a coin specialist in Philly. Liam threw his head back in despair and contemplated. She needed to be seen by a doctor ASAP, but how was he supposed to pull this off? Last time he dropped her at a hospital she ran away, living on the streets out of a tent and had ended up being attacked.

Coming home to her cooking for him and making him laugh was the most wonderful feeling his heart had ever produced. He barely knew her but with her by his side, everything became more bearable. He would do everything in his powers to help her. Whatever it would take, he would make things right again. Help her. Protect her. He just had to be careful how to approach it. Be kind about it, understanding, tell her that he cared about her, which he truly did—a lot. Taking a deep breath, Liam walked back into the living room, placing the laptop on the table as he watched Isabella putting the plates away. He gathered his courage.

"I was wondering…do you have a minute?"

She turned around, looking first at the laptop and then at him. Her hands clenched together, pressed to her chest as she took a step closer. Did she know what was coming? For a second she looked frightened, but then she nodded her head as if she had just made peace with something.

"Just promise me that I won't end up in a mental institution." Her gaze held steady on the floor.

CHAPTER 7

It was only a matter of time until someone confronted her about her odd behavior. Being from a different century placed her at a clear disadvantage at pretending to be normal. Amongst Dan and her folks, unusual meant normal. But around people of society, she stuck out like a sore thumb, feeling the clock constantly ticking, waiting to make the slip and be sent to an insane asylum or wherever the twenty-first century sent people who insisted they time traveled. What was she supposed to tell Liam now? He stood over by the table, his gaze locked on her.

"I—" He cleared his throat. "I noticed all the open search windows about time travel on the computer…"

He paused to see if she would pick up the conversation from here. For the first time in her life, she truly didn't know what to say. Not because she wasn't cunning enough to lie, but because it felt wrong after everything he had done for her. He made her laugh like nobody else ever did. She felt appreciated and accepted for who she was. At least for who he thought she was. Somehow, she had to try to get through to him with her insane story, to tell the truth, make him believe her.

"I promise I won't send you anywhere." He spoke softly, like he was approaching an injured and scared animal, and slowly edged closer. "I'm worried, Isabella. The night we met it sounded like you had a head trauma."

Isabella bit her lip, wondering where to start. This might be her only chance to tell him what was going on. He might think her mad for sure, but he already questioned her mental state—what did she have to lose?

"There is nothing wrong with me physically or mentally, Liam." She shook her head with a desperate expression painted on her face. What she was about to tell him made her sound like a total church bell.

Liam took a step closer, brows drawn in worry. "I didn't mean it like that."

"I know. But I did. I didn't hurt my head during the carriage accident."

His face was now drawn with gloom as his shoulder sank. "You mean car accident."

"No, I mean carriage accident." Her body felt heavy, chest tightened, as she struggled to breathe. She took a step closer, inch by inch until she now stood next to Liam. Her hands curled into tight fists as if to give her strength.

"The night you found me, I was involved in a carriage accident. I had the most unfortunate disagreement with my mother, and before I came back to my senses, I was hit by a carriage."

She swallowed the lump in her throat as her eyes lingered toward the open window, wanting to fly away. But he needed to hear the truth.

"Instead of waking up in 1881 London, I woke up in America, and you were holding me in your arms." Her gaze now focused on Liam. His face hard to read, like stone. "I know this sounds like utter nonsense—but it is the truth."

Liam shook his head in despair. "Isabella, we need to get you to a doctor ASAP."

"No!" Her heart sank, falling out of place. He tried to reach for her but she took a step back. "You promised."

"Not that kind of doctor. I'm talking about a medical doctor." He waved a hand in front of her. "Isabella, listen to me—"

"You're the one who's not listening. There is nothing wrong with my head. I have no idea how or why, but I came here from the past."

She placed a hand into her pocket and fished out the very coin that in her eyes was the culprit of it all. And before he could even say another word, she grabbed his wrist and turned his palm up to place the coin in it.

"Here. That's from my time. From 1881."

Liam held the coin close to his face and, for a moment, studied the object. Then subtly tilted his head, eyes closed, a clear sign that she had not got through to him.

"Isabella...please—"

"I don't know how to prove it to you, but it's the truth. I understand if you want me to leave now." Her voice quivered, reflecting the desperation that had formed inside her heart. Tears flowed from her eyes. The last few weeks had taken their toll. And now she was about to lose the man who, for some reason strange reason, seemed to mean a lot to her. After this, how could he still want to help her or stand by her side? She sounded insane!

But instead of turning away, as she'd anticipated, Liam moved closer, placing himself right in front of her. She instantly felt a warm fluttering in her stomach, unsure what to expect from him next.

"Please don't cry." He gently ran his finger over her cheek, wiping a tear away. "I won't send you anywhere, you hear me? You make everything more bearable in my life. I didn't even know I could feel this happy."

Isabella slowly tilted her head to meet his deep, arresting gaze. His were the kindest eyes she had ever seen. She was hypnotized by them, without knowing what, left her wanting more. Liam slowly leaned in, close enough for her to feel his breath, as she felt a gentle caress down her back.

"You—don't—want me to—leave?" she whispered out of breath, her heart hammering against her chest.

His lips slowly tilted toward hers.

"No...," he whispered back. And before she could say another word, his lips brushed over hers, sending burning shockwaves down her spine. His kiss deepened, spreading her lips apart, gently stroking her tongue with his. She was utterly defenseless, as if some other woman was in control of her body. She pressed herself against him, longing to feel every inch of his muscular, hard body. He wrapped his arms around her, moaning against her lips.

"Isabella..."

Never had she felt anything like this before. Granted that she had never been touched by a man this way either—that would have been deemed highly improper for an unmarried lady of her former stature—but from what she had heard from her mother and from other women, intimacy was of no pleasure for a woman at that time. But by God, if this wasn't pleasure, then what was? Her whole body was aching in places she didn't know could ache. Her back arched to feel his manhood in between her legs, longing for its touch against her body. She could feel his heart wildly beating against her breast as he breathed heavily against her lips. A mix of curiosity and lust drove Isabella as her hand slowly slid down his abdomen, sinking into his pants. He twitched underneath her gentle touch. Gosh, she wanted this man more than she ever wanted anything in her life. But just when she was about to satisfy the thirst of her wants and curiosity, a loud, vibrating sound startled her. It was Liam's phone.

She instantly tore herself away from him, tumbling backwards in embarrassment as if the phone was the reincarnation of her mother, who would have been outraged by her current behavior. Liam shuffled a few steps back, like he was just caught doing something incredibly inappropriate.

"I'm so sorry…" He stared at Isabella for a few seconds before turning around, hastening away toward the table to catch whoever called him in the untimeliest manner.

"Hello? Yes."

Isabella watched as he stood over the table, his phone held against his ear. Her stomach was still filled with trapped butterflies wanting to tear her open just by staring at him. My goodness, he was so incredibly handsome. Listening to whoever was on the phone, she saw him peek over to see what she was doing. She stood there, paralyzed with her back against the kitchen counter. Another hot flush crept across her cheeks, and she instantly turned around to dedicate herself to the dishes like nothing had ever happened.

"Are you serious? Why the hell would he offer that now? Months after endless legal battles and appeals?"

Isabella tried not to listen, but it was almost impossible considering the size of the flat she shared with the man who had just passionately kissed her. *Oh, how life has changed for you, Isabella.*

By now she was well aware that women in the twenty-first century, unlike women in her own time, were not sexually oppressed or merely considered objects with a price tag on it. But that didn't mean that she could just throw off the chains of her oppression overnight. By now she had seen many couples in the streets, kissing openly, holding hands, whispering sweet words into each other's ears. And each and every single time she blushed, turning away. In her mind she felt wicked, like she had just done something terrible. Liam's voice tore her out of her thoughts again.

"I get why you're against it, but I still have to try. I really have no choice at this point. Tell him I'll be there." Liam hung up.

What now? Isabella didn't feel like she had it in her tonight to discuss any of the plethora of difficult subjects thickening the air in the room. She didn't trust herself any longer either. If Liam triggered that tingling again, who knows what she was willing to give him. And what would he think of her then? Most certainly promiscuous. An insane wagtail. No, she'd had enough for today. She put the dried plates in the cupboard and turned to face Liam. He stared at his cell, rubbing the back of his neck before noticing Isabella's gaze on him.

"I—I didn't mean to intrude."

"It's all good. That was my lawyer. The CEO of the company that we are up against wants to meet with me."

Isabella shifted her weight, unsure what this meant. She knew that Liam was fighting to keep his business out of the hands of a big corporation, but she didn't know all the details.

"Is that good news?"

"I honestly don't know. My lawyer said that the new judge assigned to my case is a veteran and has a daughter in the military, so I assume that they are worried about him taking a liking to me and might throw a new offer. Ideally, maybe even get all their dirty little tricks out on the table. We'll have to see." He turned toward her, watching her with an intense stare.

"Isabella, about—" There it was, the beginning of the conversation she did not want to have.

"If you don't mind," she interrupted him, "I'll retire now. I feel awfully tired." She stormed past him into the bedroom before he could say another word.

Leaning against the door from the other side, she listened quietly for a moment to see if he would follow her, but for some reason he didn't. She could hear him pull out a chair. Most likely to work on the computer. Closing her eyes, she let out a hard sigh. What a mess. If only Dan was here, she'd certainly know what to do. She had that brilliant gift to call things out for what they truly were. Isabella dragged herself over to the mattress, slumping down onto it in despair.

This was going to be another sleepless night, filled with uncontrollable thoughts running through her head, turning her mind into a busy train station once more. She tried to look out the window, but from her mattress, it didn't have a view of the evening sky. Instead she was looking at the façade of another house, deep in thought, wondering why her, wondering how, wondering what she should do next. Her research on the internet had given her more questions than answers. Most of the sites about time travel were utter nonsense, bringing aliens and devil worshipers into the equation. The only comfort she found was googling her brother, George Astley, Duke of Aberdeen. There wasn't a lot of information about him or their mother personally, but his lineage continued to this day, which meant he had married at some point. Was he happily married? Did he ever stop looking for her? Didn't that mean she had family, even in this time? Could she even call them family considering the circumstances? And if things weren't already complicated enough, she had to add romance on the top of the list. Did Liam still think fondly of her, or now think of her a ninny?

"What a mess," she mumbled to herself as her eyes flickered, and her mind drifted. "What a bloody, bloody mess indeed…"

Liam awoke with a horrible stiff neck. It was barely bright out. His head buried in his folded arms, he realized that he must have fallen asleep while sitting at the table. He stretched his arms and legs, trying to get rid of that awful stiffness. The laptop sat open beside him, pushed aside just barely enough to make room for his head. Rubbing his eyes, everything slowly came back to him. The things Isabella had said about time travel, the call from the lawyer, their passionate kiss… Everything.

The memory made his throat run dry again in frustration that was directed at no one but himself. What the hell was he thinking? Isabella had just suffered from a traumatic brain injury that he was responsible for, and to top it all off, she was here to hide from a pervert. So he had nothing better to do than make a move on her? Who the hell was this man? Not the Liam he knew, for sure. The usual Liam would never have acted like a testosterone-filled youngster who can't control his emotions.

Granted, Isabella had this effect on him, like no other woman had ever before. Her smile, her eyes... He loved listening to her stories, and by God her soft lips tasted like heaven. It broke his heart to see her cry, scared to death that he might throw her out. He just wanted to comfort her, hold her, kiss her worries away. But those were excuses, not a valid reason for such shameful behavior.

He had to make things right again. All night he endlessly googled head injuries and how to help people with delusions. Considering her circumstances, he also searched for long-term furnished rentals, until his brain completely shut down on him. He wanted to offer her a way out from his place. To give her the power to choose. It wasn't until the warm sun was breathing down on his skin that he noticed a search window he'd forgotten to close last night. It was about the Astley family, one of England's finest houses. There was no doubt in his mind that this was her family. Upon close inspection, the resemblance between her and them was uncanny. But then, how did she end up here in Philly? And how was she related to the current Duke of Aberdeen? Father? Brother? Husband perhaps!

It didn't matter. If he wasn't able to get Isabella to a doctor, who knows what would happen to her.

She might get worse; things could escalate again. She might sneak away in the middle of the night, frightened of being admitted to a mental institution. Then he might lose her forever. He vowed to make things right. Today he would make her an offer she couldn't refuse.

CHAPTER 8

M uch to Isabella's surprise, Liam was still at home when she got up. She heard a clanking noise which she guessed must be from the kitchen, considering the sweet and almost buttery aroma that seeped into the bedroom. Slipping into her jeans and comfortable wool sweater, she slowly turned the knob and pushed gently enough to take a peek, testing the waters before coming out.

"Good morning. I made us breakfast."

Liam smiled from the kitchen. He was wearing a white apron, which instantly made her giggle. Never ever had she seen a man in an apron before. She walked over to the table, which set up beautifully. Not as over the top elegant as hers had been the night before, but charming nonetheless. There were several bowls filled with jam, cheese, eggs, and fruits. The smell of steaming fresh coffee filled the air and in the middle were two plates with pancakes on them.

Her cheeks flushed as she laughed, noticing the smiley faces on the pancakes made from fruits and whipping cream. Never had she seen anything like this before. Pancakes with faces, prepared by a tall, strong man like Liam. He walked over with a grin on his face.

"I hope you're not making fun of my world-famous man-cakes." His brows were intentionally drawn together making a fake angry face.

"They're the most incredible thing I've ever seen."

In some ways, it was true. Out of all the marvels of the twenty-first century, these *man-cakes* somehow managed to top it all. She pulled her chair out and sat down. Liam did the same.

"It's just... I have never seen a man make pancakes before. Actually, I'm afraid I have never seen a man cook—at all."

"Then you have never seen a real man," Liam announced, lifting his head proudly and pointing at the writing on his white apron.

This is a Manly Apron

For a Manly Man

Doing Manly Things

Isabella burst out into laughter again, holding on to the table for support. Tears of joy formed in her eyes. How did this man do it? How did he manage to make her laugh with such ease, and make her feel so carefree? His eyes watched her with a face of *mission achieved* from across the table. It took a while to calm down enough to start eating, but much to her surprise, the food tasted immaculate. Incomparable to that ungodly thing she'd somehow managed to summon on a plate the other night. For the first time since she'd arrived in America, she actually ate something that was better than what the cook at the Astley estate used to prepare for her.

"Splendid," she complimented him, leaning back in her seat after taking the last bite of her pancake.

"I know, I know," he responded with a smile, placing the palm of his hand on his heart.

"Where did you learn to cook like this?"

"In the military. The food was awful. Not as bad as yours," he said teasing her, "but still pretty terrible."

A relaxed smile crossed her face.

"Be careful, I can kill with my food." Liam shared her happy glance. That warm feeling was all around her again, inside and out. It was incredible how much she liked this man. Never had she had less in her life than now, but at the same time she was richer than ever before. She grabbed a few empty dishes but Liam got up and took them out of her hand.

"I got this. This is still part of my manly duty." He rushed into the kitchen and back to make sure she couldn't grab any other dishes.

"Are you almost ready to head out?" he asked, rinsing off a plate in the sink.

"Head out to where?"

"To the coin specialist. His shop opens at nine."

Her mouth fell open in disbelief. Did he just say the *coin specialist*?

"Coin specialist?" she repeated. Liam turned off the faucet and dried his hands on his apron.

"Yes. Didn't you say last night that you wanted to go to one? To have your coin checked?"

This was such a surprise to her that it made her stutter.

"Y-Yes. I did indeed —"

She took a step closer, shaking her head in confusion.

119

"But last night, didn't you say —"

Say what? That he didn't believe you traveled here from 1881? What if he still thought she had a head injury? She felt tense. Somber thoughts crawled their way back into her mind. She had to be careful with everything she was about to say. Perhaps even pretending it was just a joke? No, Liam was no fool to believe such a thing.

"Well, I thought we could go check it out. Nothing to lose there. But if it turns out to be a disappointing visit, maybe we could give the doctor a try. Just in case?"

He took off the apron and folded it, trying to look like they were having the most normal conversation in the world. Isabella was stunned. Amazed. Not out of anger, but in disbelief at how much this man had done for her, must care for her. Growing up with a mother who loved her jewels more than her own children, she had never had the luxury of feeling annoyed with overbearing parents. This was all new to her. Standing in front of a person who tried everything in his power to help her made her cheeks flush in embarrassment. Tongue-tied, heart swelling, not knowing what else to do, she spoke before knowing what was going to come out.

"Fair enough," she said and nodded in agreement like it was a business deal.

Liam looked surprised. "Really?"

"Why not? I mean who knows. Perhaps there is something wrong with my head." It was certainly possible. She had to look at all her options to try to understand her mysterious case as long as they did not involve the ninny house. And if it turned out in the end that she really was *non compos mentis* — unsound in her mind — would that really be the end of the world? The answer was no. She would rather be insane with no money and have Liam by her side than be rich and married to a bloody fopdoodle like Lord Warrington.

With a mutual nod between them, the deal was finalized. Isabella thought to look at herself in the bathroom mirror just to be sure she was ready, staring at the clothes that Dan had bought for her. For a brief moment, she thought of Dan and how she was doing at her friend's place right now. Was she well? How were the cats? She wanted to see her as soon as possible once everything was settled.

She poked her finger through a small hole in the sleeve of her sweater. It had obviously started to resemble the sweater of a person who had lived on the streets. Liam offered several times to take her shopping, but she had fought him tooth and nail not to let him buy things for her. She couldn't possibly ask for more than he already provided for her.

"You look terrible," she mumbled to herself, trying to fix her hair. Since she had moved in with Liam, she had taken great care over how she looked, especially since Liam looked so dashing in his suit that he wore to work every morning.

She snapped out of it, pressing her palms to her cheeks as her lips pouted like a goldfish.

"You are not here for romance!" She closed her eyes, taking one big gulp of air before staring at herself in the mirror for one last time.

"Much better," she whispered. Then she smiled. Putting on her worn-out sneakers that sat next to the bed, she tried to show as much pride as possible.

Liam was waiting for her next to the entrance door. He was also wearing jeans and a sweater, but his looked new. With confidence in her voice and hope for the future, as well as the past, she spoke.

"Ready when you are."

The coin shop was called Things Finer. It was tucked away in a small side street in downtown Philly that got barely any of the morning sunshine, which made the street look a little dark and gloomy. They got lucky and managed to park right in front of it, getting a clear view of the windows that were filled with coins in glass vitrines. By now Isabella was somewhat used to cars, although they still scared her at times considering how fast they could move.

Liam opened the shop's door for her like the gentleman he was. It felt nice to know that even after more than a century, chivalry wasn't dead. They both agreed how delightfully elegant it was inside. The ceiling and walls were made of pristine oak wood, which glistened like glass and allowed the artificial lighting inside to bounce across every inch of the room, turning the coins into sparkly stars. She knew from her own time that there were plenty of wealthy people willing to pay a high price for rare coins and antiques. A movement from a doorway caught her attention. It was a shaggy, grey-haired, long bearded old man in a suit walking toward them.

"May I help you?" he said.

"Yes," Isabella said, walking up to the vitrine he stood behind. "I was hoping you could take a look at a coin for me."

She pulled her shilling out of her jeans pocket. Liam, who was browsing the shop a moment ago, joined her by her side. Isabella placed the coin onto the glass countertop.

"I sure can."

The man leaned over with his beard touching the counter, squinting with one eye while the other one widened.

"Let's have a closer look, shall we?"

The shop owner pulled out a pair of thin, round glasses from underneath the countertop. For some reason he didn't put the glasses on, but simply held them in front of his eyes.

"Hmmm…" He picked up the coin, holding it between his thumb and index finger and against the ceiling light as if he was staring at a diamond.

"Weird…" He was scratching his head with a dazed look on his face, then shifted his gaze to Isabella. "Where did you get this coin?" he asked, turning the coin several times.

"Inheritance," Liam said before Isabella could respond.

"Will you excuse me for a moment?" The man disappeared through the doorway just to pop back out again, now followed by a tall, skinny man in his forties.

"Sorry about that. This is my son, Benjamin. I just wanted him to take a second look at this."

The old man handed the coin to his son who, just like his father, held the coin against the light. Both of them seemed intrigued.

"Is there something the matter?" Isabella tilted her body over the vitrine, trying to get a better look, curious to see what had caught their attention.

Benjamin laid the coin on a dark-blue satin cloth on top of the vitrine. From underneath the countertops, he pulled out some sort of a lamp and placed it over the coin. It lit up the coin, engulfing it in a bright white light.

"To be honest, I have never seen anything like it…"

Benjamin was now scratching his head, just like his father.

"What do you mean?" Liam stepped in to get a better look as well.

"Here." Benjamin handed Isabella a magnifying glass.

She grabbed it and leaned over the coin with it. "You see," Benjamin said and pointed at the coin, guiding her gaze toward the top edge of it. "This is an 1881 Victorian 'Young Head.' A shilling with Queen Victoria on it. There is no doubt about it. I've held hundreds of those in my hands before."

He pursed his lips into a contained smile like he was proud of it.

"Okay, so…?" Liam wondered about the "but" that had to follow soon, considering the fuss the father and son were making here.

"But…here is what makes absolutely no sense."

Benjamin pulled another coin out of the vitrine and placed it next to Isabella's. They looked identical in size and shape, but the colors of the two coins were totally different.

"This is an 1884 German Mark coin. Those two coins are identical in weight, size, and silver content."

Isabella looked up at Benjamin. "But they look so different…"

Benjamin's father stepped in. "Precisely why it makes absolutely no sense. The Young Head should have similar tarnish stains to the German Mark."

Liam now raised his eyebrows.

"But look. The Young Head looks brand new. Not the slightest scratch or tarnish. No matter how well you take care of a coin, there will always be some sort of discoloration. It's inevitable. It's the course of time." Benjamin chuckled in amusement.

"This makes no sense. I have never seen anything like it." His father nodded in agreement.

"Is the coin real? Possibly fake?" Liam asked, which made Isabella for a moment look at him a certain way. Benjamin, on the other hand, seemed offended.

"Sir, I have held thousands of fake coins in my hands before, and I can tell this to you. This one is a legit 1881 Young Head." Benjamin now crossed his arm to his chest. "I happen to know a thing or two about coins, you know."

"Yes, of course. We never doubted that," Isabella said with a warm beaming smile from cheek to cheek, breaking the tension which had made Benjamin somewhat flustered. He took the coin back in his hand, looking confidently cool with a touch of swag.

"I agree with my father. This coin is real. But you are more than welcome to have the silver tested. This coin is 92.5% silver, unlike today's coins. I bet my shop that it will come back as Heathrow silver, a mine in the north of Scotland that has long been shut down."

Liam's hand twitched in disbelief. Undeterred, he asked just to be sure.

"But what if somebody melted another coin and made a new one from the same silver?"

Benjamin handed the coin back to Isabella.

"A forgery?" His gaze shifted to Isabella who seemed displeased. "It would be close to impossible to replicate this exact print pattern to this level of perfection. The effort and money that would have to go into it... I doubt anybody would go to that much trouble. As I said, it's highly unusual to see a coin like this. In this condition, it's worth a fortune."

"There is nothing like it," Benjamin's father chipped in. "It's almost like it leapt through time," he joked with a big grin.

Isabella smirked with a slight "I told you so" look on her face as she peered over to Liam, who seemed to struggle to grasp all of this. She knew why. He brought her here to be told that her coin was just a regular collector's item. He brought her here to get her one step closer to the doctor's office. A step further away from the crazy idea of time travel. In his eyes, all of this must be going horribly wrong.

"Thank you. I really appreciate your help," Isabella said, sliding the coin back into her pocket.

"Would you consider selling it? Name any price, I'll pay it," the owner said with bright eyes, eager to hear her response. Money was a struggle for her right now. She hated the fact that she had to live off of other people's kindness. However, selling the coin was beyond unwise. What if there was more to it? This coin was the only thing that tied her to her own time, besides her dress and the jewelry set she had given Dan, who still argued with her over it as she refused it as payment for her clothes and insisted she was safekeeping it for her.

"I'm afraid I am very attached to the coin. It was my mother's —" The memory hit her like a carriage speeding down the road at full speed, literally. For a moment her heart stopped. Her throat felt rusty and her mind was running in circles again.

"I understand," Benjamin said, pulling her out from the murky depths of her mind. "But please come back to us first if you ever consider selling." He nodded with pursed lips that contained his disappointment.

"I will. Thank you again for your time." Isabella and an awfully quiet Liam walked out of the shop. She didn't dare to look at him. She wondered what was going through his head right now. He must be as confused about all of this as she. At least now she was certain she wasn't insane. For the past few days, her mind had started to waver. But now she could finally put that to rest and focus on the most important part. How in the world did she get here?!

Liam opened the car and got in. Isabella took a deep breath before joining him inside. There was thick air around them, suffocating both of them, demanding to be cleared away.

"Liam, I'm sorry." That's all she was able say.

He let out a heavy sigh. Wide eyed, he shook his head while staring out of the side window.

"There is nothing you have to apologize for. I just don't understand…"

Isabella leaned toward him.

"I don't understand any of this either. I really don't. One moment I was in my time, the next I was here, with you."

She caught a glimpse of his face from the side mirror. His lips were pressed together, eyes furrowed. He was utterly lost. Isabella hated seeing him like that. She would do anything to get him out of this state of desperation. And she knew just the thing to do that.

"Let's go to the doctor's office to get me checked out."

Why not? He promised he would never admit her to a mental asylum. To Isabella, there was absolutely no reason not to trust him. The doctor would check her out and who knows, might even have some answers to this cryptic puzzle. In the farthest reaches of her mind there was still a chance that she was hallucinating. But Liam did not react the way she had thought he would. Instead of enthusiastically starting the car, he just kept staring out the window.

"No," he said as he finally started the car. Isabella couldn't be more confused.

"No?" she asked carefully.

"Not yet. There's somewhere I want to go first," he said with determination, backing the car out of its parking spot.

"I'm afraid I don't understand." Isabella was now the one lost for words. "Where are we going?"

Liam's voice was uncertain while his gaze fumbled toward her, searching for something, before narrowing his eyes back on the road. His jaw was set as he decisively steered the car across the road before finally speaking out his mind.

"We are going back to 5th street, the street where we first met."

CHAPTER 9

None of this made any sense. How could a simple mission like this go so horribly wrong? All night he had researched how to help Isabella with her delusions, and now things were worse than they had been before. He'd managed to do the one thing that all the psychology websites warned him about — he had confirmed her delusions. The little trip to the coin shop was supposed to open her eyes, make her realize that this coin was just like any other antique coin rather than a travel companion from 1881. So, when did all of this turn from hot to wildfire?

Liam glanced over to Isabella who was looking out the window, clearly avoiding eye contact. This woman thought she'd time traveled here with nothing more than her clothes, some jewelry, and that damn coin from 1881; and according to the Finer Things shop owners, at least the coin actually did. This was crazy. What was he even thinking driving to 5th Street? He should have taken her offer and gotten her straight into medical care. So why the hell was he driving to that road again?

The answer to that question was as crazy as the time traveling coin itself. *What if…* Liam mumbled to himself. He was by no means a man who believed in Santa Claus or the Easter Bunny, but what if there was even the slightest chance that Isabella was not delusional? That little visit to Finer Things had opened the door to this cryptically incomprehensible and beyond impossible chance that she actually time tr — No. No! He couldn't even say it in his mind. That's how mad it all sounded. But then… *What if.* Beyond reasonable doubt like those lawyers used to say. It had to be a hundred percent. Not ninety, not even ninety-nine. No, he had to be a hundred percent certain she wasn't from 1881.

He cared for her, more than he ever thought possible. So if there was even the slightest chance that she was not delusional, how horrible would it be that nobody believed her? To be treated insane. Far away from everything and everybody she knew. Liam was a logical man, but his eyes betrayed him, taking a peek toward her. A few blond curls hung onto the sides of her face. Her lips were full and rosy under the warm glow of the sun as he studied the intricate curves of her face. A fuzzy feeling formed in his stomach, which led to the same desire he'd felt that night when he kissed her. He forced himself to regain composure, eyes on the road, before he ended up leading both of them into another car accident.

Liam turned into 5th Street, the very place where everything had started. During the day it looked just like any other Philly rowhouse neighborhood. Trees lined up in front of houses, all painted with white front porches. There was no parking lot nearby, so he decided to pull into someone else's driveway. It shouldn't take long. He wasn't even sure if this plan of his would work. Doubt was creeping into his mind. But again, he had to be sure, and this was the way to prove it once and for all.

"What are we doing here?" Isabella asked, opening the door. Liam's gaze surveyed the neighborhood. His face meant business.

"I want to look at people's doorbells," he said as he got out of the car and walked toward the middle of the street. Confusion clearly written all over her face, Isabella followed behind him. With his hands on his hips, eyes shifted left and right like a hawk looking for prey.

"This should be about where I hit you, don't you think?"

Still confused, she stood next to him looking at the ground. Her eyes examined the road and got caught on a pot hole.

"Yes, I believe so. I think I remember this hole on the pavement." She pointed to it.

"Good." Liam turned around and walked up to a house which was the closest to the scene of the accident. It was a blue rowhouse with a white porch. Isabella followed him with curious, big steps all the way to the door. A quick glance at the doorbell revealed that this was not what he hoped to find.

"What exactly are we looking for?" Isabella wondered. He pulled out his phone and googled a picture of a Ring doorbell.

"This." He held it right in front of her face. She grabbed the phone, analyzing the picture.

"How will this help us?"

"It records everything that happens in front of the home and stores it for sixty days."

"Like a camera?"

"Yes, sort of. It's like a surveillance camera. If we get lucky, we might be able to see what really happened that night." Gosh, he was already talking to her as if she was indeed from a different time. He walked down the steps and proceeded to a porch to the left next door. Instead of following him, Isabella meandered toward the house on the right.

Liam now stood in front of a red door with a white doorbell. But still, nothing. He took a peek toward Isabella to see if she'd gotten lucky, only to find her shaking her head back at him. No dice either. It started to set in that this plan was a far cry after all. What was he even hoping to find? Liam was about to cross the street to take a look at the houses on other side when he heard Isabella shout.

"Here! This one has the same rectangular thing like the one on your phone!" She yelled ecstatically. Liam's mouth gaped open, he staggered a step backwards as if his heart had just punched right through his chest. He couldn't believe it. He ran over to the small brick house that Isabella stood in front of, but before he could even say a word, the door opened revealing a square-faced man in his forties with saggy cheeks and droopy eyes that squinted at them.

"Can I help you?" This man was clearly not in the mood for people yelling in front of his door.

"Yes, so sorry about all of this." Liam stood next to Isabella. "We were wondering if we could take a look at your doorbell footage?"

The man scanned them from head to toe. Awkward silence filled the air. Without a word, the man slowly backed inside and was about to slam the door when Isabella placed a hand against it.

"I'm so terribly sorry for this inconvenience. We didn't mean to intrude. But I was hit by a car a few weeks ago and was hoping to find out more about what happened."

The guy was clearly thinking as he stalled for a moment. His eyes wavered while his mouth was downturned; an odd pained expression painted his face.

"My wife was hit by a car once. That asshole drove off and got away with it." He winced before finally swinging the door open, giving them a glimpse into his living room. "Come on in, I hope I can help you find that asshole."

Liam stiffened, pulling at his collar, trying to clear his throat.

"That asshole would be me," he whispered just loud enough for Isabella to hear.

"Thank you for helping me find this *asshole.*" She glanced at Liam, holding her laughter under pursed lips.

The man led them inside and into a quite cozy living room. White walls, new hardwood floors, and warm gold furniture revealed a rather tasteful and modern home. It was beautiful. Houses in this street must be expensive, Liam thought to himself.

"I'm Jesse, by the way."

"Isabella."

"Liam."

He signaled them to take a seat on the couch. "Let me grab my Mac. You guys just got lucky. My wife made me get this camera about five weeks ago. Our neighbors had noticed some creep wearing all black lingering around here at night." Jesse disappeared into the hallway.

Liam sat down next to Isabella. "Times are not what they used to be," he said in a raised voice so Jesse could hear him from wherever he was.

He came back with a laptop in his hand.

"True that. When I was a kid, I was able to play outside with my friends. Can't do that anymore these days." He placed the laptop on the coffee table in front of them. "Let's see. When did that guy hit you?"

Liam and Isabella stared at each other.

"About three weeks ago," said Liam.

Jesse opened a tab and logged into his doorbell online account. "We should be good then. They save all the footage for sixty days. So..." He browsed over a plethora of videos. "That would have been Tuesday then?"

"Thursday. It happened on Thursday," Liam said, tensing his muscles. He felt a tingle in his fingers like he always did when he was nervous. A habit straight out of the military. All the *what-ifs* were running through his head again. Isabella was obviously anxious as well. He felt her leg judder against his.

Jesse pulled up a list of dates and clicked on a video titled *Thursday, 11/03*. The screen of the laptop played a video of the street that started at the early morning hours of that day.

"This must be it. Any idea what time it happened?"

"Probably right before midnight," Liam said.

"Ok." Jesse fast-forwarded through the daytime footage. Isabella was now holding onto

Liam's arm, fingers buried onto his skin, eyes glued to the screen. His other hand reached out to give hers a gentle squeeze. No matter what they found out from this, he'd be there for her.

And in an instant, on the pitch-black screen during midnight, a car zoomed in, spreading daylight into the night, and suddenly stopped with a woman laid on the ground in front of it. They saw the entire incident in a blink of an eye.

"Wait! There it is. Go back," Liam shouted, holding his breath.

Jesse rewound the video and stopped at around 11:35 p.m. For the first few seconds, there was absolutely nothing to see. It was an empty street lit up by street lanterns. Then, all of a sudden, a red-haired woman with a long dress walked onto the street.

"Who is that?" Liam asked.

"I—I have absolutely no idea," Isabella's voice trembled. Both of them leaned closer to the screen, their faces now inches away from it.

The woman stopped in the middle of the road, seemingly staring at something on the ground. Then she bent over, reaching for something.

"What is she doing?" Jesse asked now as curious as Liam and Isabella. "I don't know. It looks like she's picking up something—"

"THERE!" Isabella shouted, pointing at Liam's car pulling around the corner. It was clearly him. His headlights lit up the whole street, putting the unknown red-haired woman into the bright spotlight. She was very attractive and must have been in her early thirties. But right there and then, the video flickered with an audible and somewhat painful white noise that made all of them squint. The next clear picture showed Liam holding Isabella. All three stared at the laptop with their mouths wide open.

"What the hell was that?" Jesse was the first to ask.

He rewound the video to the same spot where the unknown woman appeared. Liam was frozen, Isabella's arms folded onto herself, hugging herself with her fingernails breaking into her skin. They watched the scene again, but the footage remained the same, with the exact identical order of events. An unknown red-haired woman stood in the middle of the road bending over, Liam's car pulled into the street, the footage flickered followed by that irritating white noise before finally being presented with Liam holding Isabella in front of his car. The mysterious woman was nowhere to be found.

"I—I d-don't understand—" Liam stuttered, then noticed Isabella was squeezing all the blood out from her arm. He held her wrist to calm her down.

Jesse stood up abruptly and turned toward the two of them.

"What kind of a sick joke is this? What's going on here?"

Isabella managed to tear her gaze away from the laptop.

"I don't know," she answered, wildly shaking her head in disarray.

"That man in the video is clearly you!" Jesse aggressively pointed at Liam. "You're the asshole who hit her. And what did you do to the other woman?" he shouted in a threatening voice.

"What?!" Liam jumped up from his seat. He knew that the video would reveal him as the driver at some point, which would inevitably lead to confusion, but by no means did he ever imagine it would make him look like a kidnapper of someone whom he had never even met. Even worse, this incomprehensible footage meant he was the last person to see this red-haired woman before she magically vanished into thin air, leaving an unconscious Isabella behind.

"I didn't do anything to her! I don't even know this woman!" He stood. There with nothing more to say. He was utterly speechless.

Isabella got up as well. "It's true, we have never met this woman," she said with a trembling voice, pointing at the screen.

Jesse took a step back, separating himself from the two. "Why the hell would you even want to see a video that showed you hitting someone with a car?"

His statement made Liam look like an idiot. But Jesse didn't even begin to scratch the surface as to why he was so desperate to see this footage. It was supposed to prove a point. To find some clarity. To end all confusion about time travel.

"Listen, we are terribly sorry for all of this. But we just wanted to see if the car actually hit her." Everything sounded totally unbelievable. It was time to go.

"Wait a minute. Are you the creep in black?!" Jesse took a step toward Liam, his fists clenched and ready.

"Jesus! No! If you watch the whole video, you'll see that I'm actually the guy who beats him up!"

"It's true, he saved me," Isabella said stepping in front of Liam as if she was defending him.

"After nearly hitting you with his car?" He chuckled, seemingly unconvinced. It was another truth. Things were getting out of hand, everything sounded crazier by the moment.

"We better go," Liam whispered to Isabella as he pulled her by the hand and hurried out toward the front door.

"Yeah. That's right, run! Before I call the cops," Jesse yelled after them.

Liam busted out from the front door, Isabella right behind him. They continued to stumble their way back into the streets. Jesse's shouts from behind them, barely audible, were drowned out by the sound of moving cars across the road.

"We have to get out of here," Liam said, hastening back to the car with an out-of-breath Isabella right behind him. Neither turned to look back; they kept moving forward.

Inside the car, Liam backed out of the driveway, hitting the gas pedal like he'd just fled a crime scene. Their hearts were still racing, in sync with the speed of the car driving down the road until they finally calmed down as the car cruised through the street.

Liam pulled into the relatively empty parking lot of a grocery store and put the car in park. Both of them sat there for a while, staring out the window.

"What the hell just happened...?" he wondered, unable to comprehend any of this. How did he get here? He was so certain that today would be the day Isabella would make progress in her recovery. But instead today only served to justify her story. It was totally nuts. The *what-ifs* somehow turned out to be true. He threw his hand to his head.

"How? I mean *HOW*?" He sounded like he was desperately looking for an answer.

"I really do not know," she answered, sounding just as desperate as he did. "I already told you the truth last night."

Liam looked at her with his brows closely drawn together.

"Please tell me again. Don't leave anything out."

She slightly nodded. "I was at the opera with my mother. We had a disagreement over my — engagement."

Liam swallowed the lump in his throat. "You're engaged?" he asked, feeling a sharp pain in his chest.

"No, it's not like that. I misspoke. To be more precise, my mother insisted I get engaged to the most despicable man on this planet. And I refused."

"Oh..." A huge sensation of relief spread through his whole body.

"Why the hell would she do that? That's terrible!"

Her face saddened. "Indeed it is. But my time is very different from yours, Liam. Money and status mean everything. Most women cannot choose freely whom they wish to marry. My mother had managed to spend our family's fortune into ruin. I was her last hope of maintaining her social standing and financial freedom." It sounded absolutely awful saying it out loud.

"So, she tried to marry you off to some rich, nasty asshole?"

Isabella confirmed with a soft nod. The familiar burning sensation of anger coursed through his veins.

"And he knew that you didn't want to marry him?"

Isabella nodded again.

"Oh, how I wish I could have been there. I would have straightened that worthless worm out. You don't force women into marriage. How pathetic!"

The thought of somebody forcing himself on Isabella filled his heart with rage. His fingers clenched into stone-like knuckles. Isabella placed a hand on his arm, which instantly calmed him down. It was incredible how she was able to get him from a hundred degrees to zero with a single touch. "Don't worry. I gave him a good slap across the face in front of hundreds of people right before I ran away from him." Isabella chuckled.

Liam felt a bit of satisfaction hearing that. "Good girl," he growled, which made Isabella smile. It cheered him up a bit to see her smile again, even just for a brief moment.

"I don't think my mother would agree with you on that. However, it felt pretty good, to be honest."

She stared at her hand, remembering the day she finally made a decision for herself.

"So how did you get from the opera to here?"

Her smile disappeared. "Well, after slapping that fopdoodle, I fled the opera. I just had to get away from it all. My mother followed me to confront me about my behavior. It turned rather ugly." She pulled the coin out of her pocket and stared down at it with wide, glossy eyes. "She threw this coin at me as a stern warning not to defy her. When I tried to pick it up, a carriage hit me. That's the last thing I remember happening in 1881. Then I woke up here, with you."

Liam's heart felt like someone had just squeezed it like a lemon. To hear her story, to hear her suffer like that, it was more than he could bear. He leaned over and gently placed a hand on hers. "It's all over now. They can't hurt you any longer. You don't have to go back there. You can stay here with me."

She looked up at him with big, sad eyes.

You fool. Why would she want to stay here with a poor veteran if she can live in a castle made of gold?

"I'm sorry. Of course, you want to go back to your own time. I didn't mean—"

149

"I don't want to go back," she interrupted. "I want to stay here. This world is full of the most marvellous wonders. Women are free here. They don't have to marry old, despicable men for money just to be treated like a slave."

He grabbed her hand and pulled it close to his chest. "Then don't. Stay here, with me."

She turned away, looking out the window as if she couldn't bear to look at him any longer. "I can't."

"Why not? You don't have to stay with me if you don't want to. I could pay for an apartment for you."

She gently freed her hand from his. "That's not it. It's about my brother. I can't do that to him. He must be worried sick about me."

Liam leaned back into his seat, throwing his head backwards. This whole situation was a tragic mess. Next to him was a woman as fine as they came. A good person through and through. A fighter. Selfless, strong, and decent. And how did life treat her? It forced her into a marriage with some old bastard, then took her out of her misery like some unknown magical wish to show her what real life could be, just to throw her back into her torturous existence again.

"I really don't think you should go back. I doubt your brother would want you to."

Isabella bit her lip. For a moment it looked like she was seriously considering staying. But then shook her head.

"No, I couldn't. I couldn't do that to him. He is risking his life in the Wild West mining for some gold just to save me from that horrible marriage. I could not live with myself knowing he is looking for me, never knowing what had happened. He would try to find me until his last breath."

As much as he hated it, he understood where she was coming from. The thought of losing her to the past was as painful as it was real. But then, he wasn't some man out of 1881 who treated women like property. Isabella was her own woman, free to choose her own future. It broke his heart, but he would have to do everything in his powers to help her get back home. He wanted her to be happy, even if that meant letting her go.

He looked over to her. Their eyes met, deep and longing. Before he could even try to keep his emotions under control, his stomach felt that familiar fluttering coursing down below. His heart pounded faster, captivated by her eyes. How could she be this beautiful? He couldn't help but stare at her full rosy lips. The memory of their sweet taste flooded his mind, clouding his judgement, and for a second he pictured kissing her: not only her lips but every inch of her body. Her cheeks turned red and he noticed her breath quicken. Could she tell what was on his mind? And just when he was about to give in to his desire, to lean in and kiss her like he had never kissed a woman before, he heard a voice in his head yelling. *STOP IT! SHE IS NOT YOURS! She is only passing through, and your job is to help her with that, not make a move on her*! With all the willpower a man could possibly possess, he slowly backed away.

Isabella seemed to have realized that the moment of romance had passed, and she turned her gaze to face the side window. Was that disappointment her body language was yelling at him? *It doesn't matter*. Liam backed out of from their parking spot.

"I think I know someone who can help us." He now had her attention again.

"Really? Who?" she asked with all the curiosity in the world.

"The only person I know crazy enough to be a genius."

Isabella wrinkled her forehead. "Who is that?"

"Eva...aka my sister," he said, pulling out of the parking lot and back onto the main street.

"Oh, I didn't know she was a genius." Isabella sounded impressed.

"Well, she is crazy too," Liam said as if he was mentally preparing for her.

"By the way, what is a fopdoodle?" he asked out of the blue with an eyebrow raised.

Isabella grinned. "A fopdoodle is similar to a lubberwort."

Liam grinned.

"Ooooh, yes, of course. A lubberwort... How silly of me."

It took Isabella a second to realize that he was teasing her. She threw her head back in loud laughter. "I think we need to work on your Victorian cuss words," she joked back.

"I couldn't agree more." He smirked, intending to hold her to that promise.

Denise Daye

CHAPTER 10

Eva lived in a small detached home on the outskirts of Philly. She shared her house with two other people. Much to Isabella's surprise, Liam told her that both of them were men. But neither of them were married to her or romantically involved in any way. Isabella had to remind herself, again, that this was a different time and that women were allowed to have male friends without being considered inappropriate. Besides, wasn't she living with an eligible, handsome bachelor herself?

Her cheeks flushed thinking about their kiss last night. Earlier in the parking lot, she thought he was about to kiss her again, and a proper lady would have turned away from such an intense gaze, but she couldn't. His eyes were intoxicating and when his gaze burned into her, filled with his glistening desire, she wanted nothing more than to give herself to him, no matter what he asked for. But luckily or not, it had never come to that.

Liam rang the doorbell that looked like one of those camera doorbells they saw earlier today. A woman's voice answered through it.

"Yes, who is this?" a female voice asked in a serious tone.

Liam rolled his eyes. "I know you can see me, Eva."

"Of course I can see you, but I'm not sure who you are," Eva replied.

Liam's hand brushed his hair which ended up scratching the back of his head. "Eva, stop with this nonsense."

The door stayed closed. Did his sister not know who he was? Liam waited for a second but then rang again.

"It's Liam... Your brother..." He placed his face right in front of the doorbell camera.

"You look familiar, but I haven't seen my brother in so long I almost forgot what he looked like."

Isabella's confusion turned into amusement as she realized that Eva was being sarcastic. Liam, on the other hand, was not amused at all.

"Come on, Eva, you know how busy I am."

"Ah yes. Too busy to answer your worried sister's phone calls. Too busy to let her know you're still alive, coz honestly, I thought you were dead."

Liam rolled his eyes and mumbled something even Isabella couldn't understand.

"I texted you last week." If he thought that had done the trick, he was mistaken, as Eva turned quiet behind the door. A moment of awkward silence filled the air as Liam waited for something to happen. Finally, he raised his hands in an *"I give up"* gesture.

"Alright, fine. I am sorry. I should stop by more often," he said in a sincere tone.

"And return my phone calls."

"Yes, and return your phone calls. All twenty of them."

Silence again…

"Oh come on now. That was a joke for Christ's sake. Look…" Liam dragged Isabella in front of the camera. "I brought a guest. A woman…"

It took another ten seconds or so for Eva to finally open the door and reveal herself. She was quite pretty, but dressed rather unusually. Her black hair was placed in a bun that had colorful strings twisted into it. She wore a white T-shirt with rainbow-colored loose pants. Eva scanned Isabella from head to toe.

"You get married in Vegas or something?" she asked, crossing her arms to her chest.

"No, Eva, I didn't."

"Too bad, that might have loosened you up a bit." Eva stepped aside to let them in.

Her apartment was furnished with Indian-looking wood furniture. It had colorful fabrics hanging on every wall in every room. A strong scent that was reminding Isabella of incense was filling the room with light, visible smoke, just like a church. She walked over to her phone to turn off the loud sound of a male voice repeating the words "*Suffering leads to enlightenment*" over and over again. Isabella couldn't help but throw Liam a look.

He caught it and whispered, "We call people like her *hippy*. They are like the rain. Nobody likes them but they are needed."

"Ooooh. Hippy…" Isabella nodded in fascination as if she'd just learned something extremely useful.

Eva pointed to her couch that was covered in some sort of wool blanket.

"Have a seat. Tea?"

Liam and Isabella sat down on the couch. Isabella ran her fingers through the wool blanket. It was the softest material she had ever felt. Eva noticed. "Organic fair-trade alpaca wool. It's good for your body's energy flow. Tea?"

"Erm—yes, please," Isabella almost stuttered. This place was fascinating. Her big eyes wandered to a framed diploma on the wall.

"Doctorate in Physics. From Harvard," Liam explained.

"Truly incredible," Isabella whispered, stunned. She had heard of Harvard in her own time as a university of great innovation that started to compete with Oxford in its prestige, even beat it at times.

"I told you. She's so crazy that she's a genius." He shook his head in agreement over his own words.

Eva came back with a tray carrying tea and cookies.

"Thank you," Isabella said, grabbing a cookie. She took a bite and instantly held up her hand to cover her mouth. Liam was not as polite and spat it right back out.

"What the hell is this?" He made a face as if he'd just bitten into a lemon.

"Cricket flour. It's the future. The meat and soy industry as we know it is no longer sustainable," Eva answered him calmly, putting the tray onto the coffee table in front of them. Isabella was burning to ask her for more details about this very peculiar remark and opened her mouth, but Liam elbowed her softly in her side to signal her not to.

"So, what brought you here, if I may ask? I'm Eva, by the way." She kindly smiled at Isabella, taking a seat in a chair across from them.

"Isabella. It's a pleasure to make your acquaintance."

Eva drew her brows together. "Mm-hmm. I see," she said, looking at Isabella as if she was onto something. "I guess that explains what brought you here."

Liam let out a heavy sigh. He obviously did not find Eva amusing, sister or not.

"Well, I was wondering if you could help us out. Maybe you know someone who has spent some time researching the phenomenon of time lapses."

Eva leaned over and grabbed one of her cookies. "Mm-hmm. Why?"

Her eyes stared like daggers. She was definitely suspicious. Isabella and Liam looked at each other. Eva seemed very open to the unusual, but was that enough to tell her about this predicament? Liam seemed to think it was. He took in a deep breath, and so it began.

"Isabella traveled here from far away."

"Yes, I heard the accent," Eva said, taking a bite of her awful cookie. "But?" She nudged Liam to continue.

Was he really going to tell her? Just like that? He took in another deep breath, patting Isabella's leg to assure her everything was okay before staring back daggers at his sister.

"But from a different time."

The cookie Eva held to her mouth fell from her hand as she stumbled to catch it before it fell on the floor. Regaining her composure, she surveyed Isabella from head to toe for the second time.

"Say it again?" Her dagger-like eyes shifted into glimmering sun beams as her pupils dilated, now staring closely at her brother.

"Yes, I know it sounds crazy, but she is from 1882."

"1881," Isabella corrected him almost in a whisper, realizing how insane they both sounded.

"So, you're saying she time traveled here from 1881?" Eva closed her eyes, took in a deep breath and held it.

That indeed made her sound like a ninny. Liam and Isabella looked at each other, then shifted their gaze back to Eva who still had her eyes closed, then back at each other. The anticipation felt like forever.

"Ok, I believe you," Eva suddenly said, letting out all the air.

"Really?!" They both shouted with a dazed look on their faces.

"Sure, why not." Eva shrugged her shoulders. "My brother is known for his lack of belief. For him to make such a claim can only mean that he has already exhausted all possible and viable options. And according to the latest studies, it's not that impossible anymore to harness the power of quantum mechanics to place humongous objects, like planets and stars, into a state of superposition."

All Isabella heard were mumbled words which made no sense. They both stared at Eva with half-shut eyes and wrinkled foreheads. Eva rolled her eyes as if she was talking to little children.

"In other words, time travel is now considered possible."

Isabella clapped her hands in excitement that made her jump to her feet.

"I knew it!"

Her hands still pointed in the air, she slowly sat back down.

"I never lost faith in this world with all its intelligent people and marvelous inventions! What machine do we use to get me back in time?"

She looked at Eva with puppy eyes. Eva rubbed the back of her neck.

"I don't want to be the messenger of bad news, but time travel won't be possible in any of our lifetimes."

Eva might as well have landed a punch right into her face. It would have had the exact same effect as the words she had just delivered. A clump of painful frustration formed in Isabella's throat. "But didn't you just say that time travel is now possible?"

"In theory. Thanks to quantum physics, science is at the precipice of understanding that. However, our knowledge of it is still in its infancy. Possible does not mean feasible. It will take years to understand the very basics of it, yet alone build a working prototype of a time traveling machine." Eva noticed how Isabella's face turned into a frown.

"But if I were to use common sense, then it's obviously possible if you traveled all the way here."

Isabella clenched her teeth. This was terrible. For a moment it seemed like there was hope. For the first time since she'd traveled here, someone seemed to understand what was happening to her. But in the end, life was simply mocking her yet again. Her disappointment was scribbled all over her face with huge, bold marker ink. Liam put an arm around her shoulders to comfort her.

"We will find a way."

Then he shifted his attention to his sister.

"Eva, don't you know anybody who could help?"

Eva rubbed her chin. "It depends. How comfortable are you to try a more, shall I say, unconventional approach?"

Isabella felt Liam's hand rubbing gently up and down the side of her arm. It felt wonderful. Every spot where his hand touched lit on fire.

"I'm sitting here talking with you about time travel. Me. Your brother. Who doesn't even believe in the weather forecast."

Eva glanced over to Isabella.

"Ok. But I warned you. Don't you get all mad at me like you did on your birthday two years ago."

Liam started massaging his temple in annoyance with the hand that was not holding Isabella.

"You called a stripper for me. To my office! I had to pay her two hundred bucks just to get her to leave without taking her clothes off."

Eva crossed her arms and lifted her chin in defiance.

"Well, she liked you. I thought it would loosen you up a bit. The army had turned you from a warm, funny person to a grumpy, empty shell."

Isabella didn't believe her ears. Liam? Grumpy? That couldn't be further from the truth.

"I went to war, Eva, not Disneyland."

"Well, I thought the warm touch of a woman might wake you up again."

The way they argued, there was no doubt that they were siblings—who cared deeply for one another. In their own way, that is.

They exchanged pouting looks.

"But I see you didn't need my help after all." Eva's gaze met Isabella's eyes, then she gave her a grin.

Isabella moved in her seat, trying to look away, while Liam instantly moved his arm.

"It's not like that."

"Mmmhmm... It's like you're your old self again, little brother."

Eva smirked at them both. But before Liam or Isabella could protest again, she got up.

"That's it for today. I hate to kick you both out, but I have to leave in five minutes. I have to give a lecture about Astrophysics at UPenn."

Isabella and Liam got up as well. This was so very abrupt. Eva was truly unique.

"I thought you were going to help us," Liam asked on their way out.

"I will. Come back tomorrow. At ten a.m. sharp."

Those were Eva's last words before she closed the front door behind them. They both stood there for a moment, trying to process what had just happened. Liam took the first step walking toward his car. Isabella soon followed.

"I told you she's crazy. That's my sister, by the way. I honestly wouldn't be surprised if you forgot."

Isabella chuckled. "She's different. I like her. A lot."

"She's quite annoying, and hard to deal with at times." His eyebrows perked. "Actually, all the time." He shook his head. Isabella gave him a smirk.

"As I said, I like her."

"Why am I not surprised, Miss Astley?" He gave her a cheeky smile that made her return the favor.

"Where to next?" she said, still holding her smile.

"Home, I'm afraid. I have that dinner with the CEO tonight. I can't miss it." The smile on his face slowly faded, replaced by a huge gasp of breath. "The future of my employees depends on it."

"Of course." Isabella placed a hand on his shoulder. "You'll do great."

Liam nodded, but the smile on his face refused to come back.

"What is it?" she asked, noticing it.

"Nothing. It's just… I almost forgot about tonight. The most important moment of my life." He turned the keys as the car roared to life.

"Oh… I'm sorry. I take up all your time."

"No, no, that's not it." He shook his head, placing his hand on hers before she could pull it away. "It's more like, I don't know how to explain it, but when you're around, it's like nothing else matters. Even the worst seems bearable."

His gaze melted her heart. Feeling his warm hand on her skin made her want to slip her fingers into his, locking them in place. Nothing seemed impossible when he was with her. He would do everything for her. Now it was time to do something for him.

"That CEO tonight, what sort of a man is he?"

He seemed a bit surprised by that question. "What sort of a man? Rich prick wants to be richer type. Why?"

Isabella slowly nodded her head in approval.

"Entitled?"

"Absolutely."

"Is he used to others doing whatever he demands without questioning him, no matter what?"

"Yep. Why?" Liam's face was now curious and amused.

"May I come with you tonight?"

Liam tilted his head sideways. He thought about it for a second.

"These people are my kind of people. Please believe me when I tell you that they only understand one language."

"Which is?"

"Status." Unwelcome memories of the shallow and despicable behaviors of high society came rushing back to her. Flashbacks of a life that she was once a part of. Her own family, one of England's finest, had helped set the very tone that would divide her country into classes and oppress the poor. Once again, she felt ashamed of herself, just like when she'd first gotten to know Dan and learned what life was like on the other end of the stick. For a moment, her eyes were lost, wondering how Dan was doing.

"And you wouldn't mind?" His voice tore her out of her thoughts.

"Are you jesting? All day you have been driving me through town on the ridiculous notion that I time traveled here from 1881. This is the very least I could do. Please let me help you."

Liam pondered deeply about this plan of hers which was still left uncertain. "Well, if you really don't mind. It kind of makes sense what you're saying. And I'm at a loss on how to deal with this guy anyway. I was actually worried I might lose my temper with him. Having you around could actually help."

Her face lit up. It filled her with joy that she was finally able to repay his kindness for the first time ever—definitely not including the lethal dinner she'd tried to make.

"Splendid." Liam nodded in satisfaction over what was to come. "In that case, we have to make a quick stop."

"Where to?"

"The mall. You need a dress that suits a modern lady. And don't even try to talk me out of it again. You basically already agreed." He smiled at her.

A warm tingle was now added to the joy that was already rushing through her body. There was no way out of it. She just had to go along with it as she gave him a warm smile in reply. "If you insist."

CHAPTER 11

Liam couldn't believe his eyes when the bathroom door opened and Isabella stepped out all dressed up like that. She wore a dark blue, ankle-length cocktail dress with an embellished neckline and a sexy side slit that ran all the way from her silver high heels to a few inches above her knee. Her hair was put up into a bun, except for a few strands that hung down the sides of her face. She was wearing no makeup, but by God, she was the prettiest woman he had ever laid eyes on. Her eyelashes were naturally long and her bright blue eyes looked like a piece of the blue sky. He tried not to look at her rosy, full lips as this always got him thinking naughty thoughts.

"You look stunning," he said with his mouth gaping.

Isabella playfully turned in a circle, giving him the full view.

"Thanks." She smiled, lifting her chin in confidence as her eyes scanned Liam who was wearing a well-tailored black suit.

"You look very handsome yourself."

"Thanks." But instead of offering her his arm, he pulled a little red satin box out of his blazer pocket and handed it to her. Her eyes widened in surprise.

"What is that?" She gasped, opening it. Isabella had no idea that while she was trying on dresses, he had gone to the jewelry section of the store and bought her a pair of white gold earrings and a necklace. The set was arranged in a floral design that looked very much like it just came out from the Victorian era.

"Oh Liam…" She covered her mouth as the gold pieces sparkled under the light, reflecting into her eyes.

"You can exchange it in case you don't like it, but I thought it might remind you of home."

Isabella threw herself into his arms before realizing what she was doing. "I love it. It's the most beautiful gift I've ever received."

Liam jittered as he felt the sudden unexpected warmth of Isabella. Feeling her skin rest around his neck, his arm steered its way around her waist, holding her close. He gently lowered his head into her hair, slightly intoxicated by her sweet scent.

"I'm glad you like it," he said with his eyes closed. It might very well be one of the last items his credit card would let through before declining any further purchases, but in his eyes, it was money well spent. If this dinner didn't turn into a deal, he was done. He would most likely die with enormous amounts of debt attached to his name, so why not go down by putting a smile on a woman's face? Especially if that woman was someone he cared deeply for.

He held her for a second longer, then softly let her go. "We better go." Isabella grabbed her coat to put it on before giving Liam a cheeky grin.

"Ready for battle."

"To win the war," he joked back at her.

Liam pulled in front of the Ritz-Carlton hotel. Isabella got out first. She had never been in this part of town before. The hotel had been built with a neoclassical theme, featuring a huge rotunda. A man in a black suit and white gloves came running toward them as Liam handed him the keys to his car. Isabella recognized this simple act and instantly knew what the man was doing. They had one in their own house and called them footmen.

Liam walked over to Isabella and offered his arm. Isabella accepted it with a nod as they both entered. The entrance had two porters who instantly opened the doors for them. Much to her surprise, the elegance inside of the foyer could have passed for a luxury hotel of her own time. There were small differences in the furniture, but overall the high ceiling, golden fixtures, marbled floors, and the staff in uniforms gave her the illusion that she was back in her own time.

Liam scanned the entrance hall and led her into the rotunda. The room was a formal dining area, held with enormous pillars that decorated the walls under a high-domed ceiling, giving the impression that one was in a Greek temple.

"Do you have a reservation?" A woman dressed in black who seemed about Isabella's age approached them.

"Yes, I think it's under Brunswick," Liam replied. The woman scanned her list while Isabella realized what Liam had just said. Brunswick... *Brunswick?* It sounded so awfully familiar! Wasn't that the name of a German noble family that Isabella's family had married into in the late 1400s? For the first time in her life, she wished she had paid more attention to her awfully dry history tutor.

"This way," the woman said, leading them into a closed-off area. Their table was decorated with a white table cloth under crystal clear glasses for wine and water, with fresh white roses that rested in a silver vase. The table was set up elegantly, but not for dinner.

"I assume Mr. Brunswick has changed his mind in regards to dinner," Isabella said, sitting down on the chair Liam had pulled back for her.

"Why do you think so?" He sat down next to her.

"This table is not set up for dinner. I noticed some of the other tables were set up for dinner similarly to how it would have been prepared in my own time, but ours is not."

Liam looked over to a neighbor's table. Creases started to form on his forehead as he shook his head.

"Looks like this bastard won't even waste his time for a dinner." He let out a huge stream of breath from his nose. "He probably thinks this will be a quick meeting. In and out. Sealing the fate of so many people in less than a single drink."

Isabella wrinkled her forehead in thought. This name, Brunswick, there was no doubt. It must have been that noble family from Germany.

"*Brunswick*." She caught Liam's attention as the crease in his forehead faded away. "I believe I'm familiar with this name. Do you know anything more about him?"

"Brunswick? Not much, besides him being as arrogant as he is rich. And he happens to be a billionaire."

"Sounds like the type of man my mother would like." Isabella took a sip of water.

"Looks like I'm starting to get to know your mother already." Liam glanced over the wine card. "He has destroyed countless companies for a quick profit, leaving behind a trail of impoverished and desperate people so long it would probably wrap around the globe. His name used to be Miller, like the cheap beer. But a few years back he bought a castle in Germany that came with a title, so he changed his name."

Yes! Yes! Yes! Isabella lifted her chin up with a victorious grin. This war was won without even going into battle!

"Excellent!" she almost shouted in excitement.

Liam was obviously confused, but before he could ask her what she was so happy about, a short, skinny old man walked up to them. He wore a bright gold suit. Its glitter was distracting even from across the room.

"You must be joking…" Liam barely got out in disapproval as Brunswick glided through the dinner room, blinding other guests in his ridiculous suit. Neither Liam nor Isabella had the time to rise and greet him as Brunswick sat down without even a single word or nod. The first thing he did was arrogantly wave at a waitress, leaving no doubt that he was used to being served.

What an ill-mannered man. But at the same time this was wonderful news for Isabella. All of it. Her whole life she had lived amongst people like Brunswick; she even used to be one of them. He didn't know it yet, but Brunswick was about to get played like a violin.

"So, you brought your wife?" he said, still not looking while taking a gentle sip of water. Liam was quick to react, but Isabella was faster.

"Fiancée. I do hope I am not intruding," she replied in the most noble British tone his ears must have ever had the pleasure of hearing.

Brunswick studied her for a moment. "No, not at all," he replied, averting his gaze toward the wine list without even recognizing the server as he made his selection of preferred wine.

"I heard a British accent?"

"Indeed. Isabella Astley. It's a pleasure to make your acquaintance."

Brunswick was now closely staring at her, like he was scanning every inch of her skin. Not once had he even looked at Liam.

"The pleasure is mine, Miss Astley."

She tilted her head with a barely visible grin. "Please, call me Isabella," she said, forcing a charming tone.

"Only if you call me Tom." He made a gentle nod toward her.

"Deal, as you Americans would say," she joked in an elegant laugh. The server returned with a bottle of wine and started pouring their glasses.

"I must confess, when Liam informed me that your name was Brunswick, I could barely sleep last night."

"And why is that?" Curiosity littered all over his face, something that didn't happen too often.

"Not that it is a matter of much consequence, but our houses are related."

Tom's chest perked up and his elbows pulled back as he raised an eyebrow in a mixture of pride, astonishment, and confusion. There was no doubt in Isabella's mind that this man was nothing more than a buffoon, a pretentious fool, and she intended to exploit that.

"Brunswick of Lower Saxony, is it not?"

It took Tom a few moments to process her words before finally leaning over in excitement.

"Yes, that is correct! That's my estate!"

Isabella was by no means surprised that he hadn't even bothered to read up some of the history of the title he had purchased. But then, it wasn't like it was truly *his* title. This estate made him as much of a true lord as lipstick would make a pig a princess.

"Then there is no doubt. Our ancestors were married to one another in the fourteen hundreds. I admit that was quite a long time ago, but for houses as old and prestigious as ours, some might actually still think of it as relevant," she said with a slight smirk on her lips.

If a human could burst out of pride and arrogance, Tom Brunswick would have done so at this very moment.

"Yes, I've heard of that," he said, now with a visible grin on his face that made him look foolish. *What a liar.* "So, you *are* part of the British nobility?"

Holding the wine glass in between her thumb and index finger, Isabella took a gentle sip that emphasized her rosy red lips. Then she leaned closer to him and whispered, "One does not talk about it openly these days, but like yours, my family dates back centuries."

Tom lengthened his neck like a rooster that had just been crowned king of the hen house.

Isabella held her laughter under tight lips as she peeked over at Liam who was watching the whole thing like he was in the first row of a movie theater. She could tell by the faint smile on his lips that he knew what sort of man Tom Brunswick truly was. But there was something else in Liam's face. The way he looked at her… Was it admiration?

"I can't believe that we met just like this. All those years have passed, and finally our families have met once again. It's almost like fate brought us together," Tom announced with a sparkle on his face.

"Splendid indeed." Isabella smiled back. "However, I must confess," she said as her tone suddenly changed, "I was rather anxious over the thought of our families meeting again under such dire circumstances."

His face turned weighty.

"But then I am relieved for us to have met before the Queen's invitations had proceeded for her annual hunting celebrations. She is so very particular about whom she invites. Although the estate of Brunswick has received an invitation for centuries, this one is held in honor of the veterans you see…"

Isabella took another sip of her wine. The ball was now in Tom's court. His eyes simply stared at her. The momentary silence was growing painful for him. He cleared his throat and coughed to gather his voice.

"I couldn't agree more. I'm so glad we could meet to resolve this *ridiculous* misunderstanding."

Liam almost spat out his wine but managed to hold it in by pressing his fist onto his lips, giving him an uncomfortable cough. Tom didn't seem to notice.

"People at my company can be such idiots. As soon as I heard that the owner of Green Wear LLC was a veteran, I demanded that my secretary arrange for this meeting the very next day, so I could make things right again. It was totally unacceptable how they were treating him."

Tom's attitude had changed completely. Liam stared at him like he had just seen a ghost. He struggled to speak, searching for his voice which he couldn't find. In his stunned state, a man dressed in black caught his gaze as he approached their table. The stranger bent over to Brunswick and whispered, "Sir, your car is ready."

"You idiot. Who told you to disturb me right now?" Brunswick yelled at him.

"I—I'm s-so sorry." The man looked terrified. "I thought you said to come get you in five minutes as this—"

"Are you retarded or something? Short wired? Stupid? Go wait for me outside!"

Like a beaten puppy, the man turned around, almost running back to wherever he had come from. *What a despicable creature Brunswick was!*

"I'm sorry about that." Tom shook his head as if he truly had no idea what it was all about.

A buffoon, Isabella thought to herself again. Her hand burned with desire to empty the contents of her glass in his face, but she placed a hand on Liam's arm instead and put on a fake smile.

"See, dear? Didn't I tell you this was a huge misunderstanding? Members of high society do not waste their time trying to bleed stones dry. It's beneath them, isn't that right Lord Brunswick?" Isabella asked intentionally, placing a hand to her lips. "Oh, please accept my apology. I mean Tom." She knew he was already eating out of her hand like a starved rooster, but calling him a *lord* was that little push necessary to tip the scale in Liam's favor.

"Apology accepted." He grinned while waving another waitress to come over. "Please get me a bottle of your finest champagne."

The waitress nodded and rushed off.

Liam finally found his voice. "Y-Yes...." He cleared his throat. "You did say that..."

If this had been 1881, the two men would now withdraw to discuss the details of their business agreement in the cigar room. But of course this hotel did not have such amenities, so it was up to Isabella to excuse herself for a while.

"Would you excuse me?" Isabella got up. "I shall refresh myself."

"Of course," Liam said as both men stood up.

On her way to the bathroom, she managed to peek over her shoulder to get a glance at Liam. Much to her surprise, he was staring at her, pretty much ignoring the babbling peacock sitting in front of him. She felt a touch of lightness in her limbs. It felt like she was floating. Rarely had she felt as happy as she felt now, which had been the case for the past couple of days—a streak she hoped to continue. Staring at her reflection in the bathroom mirror, she noticed something had changed. For the first time in her life, she truly liked the person she was seeing in the mirror. She had managed to do so much more than just assist a kind man whom she cared for. This simple little gesture was so much more than that. From the deepest depths of her heart, she had saved the man she loved.

It was already late when Tom finally received an important phone call that put an end to this meeting. Isabella had barely made it out of the hotel lobby when Liam grabbed her by her waist, lifted her up, and swirled her around in circles.

"Isabella Astley! You are the most magnificent person I have ever met!"

She laughed, grinning from ear to ear as he lowered her down, his hands still glued to her waist.

"It was nothing." Her cheeks felt as warm as her fast beating heart in her chest. Her skin tingled from the touch of his strong hands that held her back.

"Nothing? You saved us! My employees, the farmers…me! Thanks to you, they're all saved!"

Isabella smiled. A smile filled with awe. Never before had she seen Liam this happy. He looked like someone who had all of his worries just fall off his shoulders. They had spent another three hours talking to Tom. Not that it was a pleasure, but it was necessary to land the arrangement that would save the company. The end result was better than Liam could ever have dreamt of. Tom had called his lawyer to have a contract drafted which would sell the company's shares back at half the price that Liam's former partner Mark had sold them for. His lawyer thought him mad, but Tom insisted, yelling at him with his favorite words — "quiet" and "idiot."

"I assume there is no annual hunting party that he will be receiving an invitation to?" Liam smirked.

She grinned back at him. "Of course, there is, but I highly doubt that he'll receive one. Will you be able to get the money in time to buy back the shares? This charade will only last until he realizes that the hunting party took place without him."

Liam nodded confidently.

"Ooooooh yes. Now that I am the sole owner of the company, the bank will have no problems loaning me the money for that. The company itself has a lot of equity and earning potential. Tom was just making it seem worthless by blocking all the sales. It was a fifty-fifty ownership which meant he could have just blocked me into ruin. And he pretty much did until you showed up."

She was about to say something when she suddenly noticed all the city lights and the tall buildings that surrounded her. She had seen some parts of Philly at night before, but not the buzzing nightlife of a downtown metropolis. It was incredibly beautiful, especially for someone who came from a time where buildings were barely taller than trees, and light, besides the sun, only came from candles and gas lanterns. Intoxicated by its charm, she walked straight past Liam to the edge of the sidewalk, taking in the view.

"What is it?" Liam asked, following her.

She looked up at the skyscrapers with eyes sparkling in awe, turning her head slightly toward Liam without changing the direction of her gaze from above. "All these lights. It's as if a thousand stars were picked up from the sky and scattered across the city. It's the most beautiful thing I have ever seen."

It was incredible. Thousands upon thousands of lights, spanning across different colors, from street lamps, to buildings, traffic lights to cars, and even a huge clock from a distance; she was truly hypnotized. Liam's eyes were captivated as well, but not by the city. He looked at her as if the rest of the world had ceased to exist.

"Beautiful indeed," he murmured.

She turned toward him, catching his gaze. He stared at her so long and deep her heart nearly stopped. A warm tingle spread from her stomach, coursing through every inch of her body. In that moment in time, what she felt was crystal clear as the night sky above—it was love.

Liam took one step closer, then another, every step breaking the distance between them until he stood right in front of her. His hand brushed across her cheek and paused right beside her neck, gently tugging on one of her curls. An undeniable desire radiated between them, a desire she was willing to give so freely with everything a woman had to offer. As if he could read her mind, he leaned in, placing his face just inches away from hers, and their breathing quickened. It was intoxicating.

"Isabella," he whispered, ready to sink his beautiful lips onto hers.

She leaned her head back as her lips unconsciously parted for him, inviting his kiss to help her ease that burning desire rushing through her veins, crawling under her skin. She could feel his sweet breath, inching closer and closer, when a loud voice tore her back into reality.

"EXCUSE ME, SIR! YOUR CAR IS READY," a man shouted from behind her.

Both of them jerked around to find the valet driver frantically waving at them through Liam's car window. He was parked in front of the hotel, a long, angry line of cars waiting behind him. Liam was barely able to tear his eyes from Isabella, but a second more desperate yell from a driver stuck behind Liam's car finally did the trick. "Get out of the way!"

They both rushed over to the car. Liam fished out a few bank notes and handed them to the valet driver with an apology. The valet driver looked into his hand and seemed to be more than satisfied and gave them a nod, leaving them alone with the car.

They hurried into the car to move out of the lane and as far away from the hotel as possible. Isabella looked over to Liam, who caught her gaze with a quick, devilishly handsome smile. He didn't say a word. He didn't have to. Instead he placed a hand onto hers. Her fingers perfectly slid into his, both hands gently held together. Although they were no longer standing in front of each other ready to let their desires run loose, the air around them still lingered with love and excitement. Good God, and if it was the last thing she would do...

"I shall kiss him," she whispered, not taking her eyes off the man who not only had awoken her deepest desire but also the love in her heart.

As their car pulled around the corner, away from the Ritz-Carlton, a dark silhouette stepped out of the shadow of one of the hotel's huge pillars. His blurry eyes stared down the street they'd just turned onto. And as quick as the shadow appeared, it vanished again, melting back into the darkness where it had come from.

CHAPTER 12

uch to Isabella's disappointment, the kiss she had longed for would have to wait. She noticed a familiar police car the moment they turned around the corner. Liam saw it too.

"Did they finally catch him?" Unable to keep still, her hands were twitching nervously.

"God, I hope so. Although I would hate to see you move out again," Liam said, without a smile.

Isabella got out of the car but didn't see Jerry anywhere. Liam was right behind her, opening the front door to the apartment complex's entrance hall to find Jerry leaning against the wall next to Liam's apartment door. He was about to light a cigarette, even though it was a no smoking zone, but decided to tuck it away when he saw them coming.

"Isabella!" He acted as if he was deeply surprised to see her here. "How kind of you to fit me into your busy schedule," Jerry stated sarcastically.

Isabella rushed over to him in embarrassment. "Jerry, I am so terribly sorry. Did you wait long?"

Liam opened the door and before he could even get in, Jerry took the freedom to do so first.

"After you, Jerry." Liam stretched his arm out in a welcoming but sarcastic gesture. Jerry walked over to the table and leaned against it, crossing his arms to his chest.

"Why would you be sorry? It's only been like the fourth time this day alone that I've stopped by wondering where the hell you were without letting me know what's going on. Luckily it's not like I would have better things to do."

A flush creeped across her cheeks as her lips turned into a grimace. He had every right to be upset. She should have at least notified him of her whereabouts.

"I am incredibly, sorry. I really am. I should have telephoned you. Today was just..." Her gaze momentarily shifted to Liam. "I was incredibly busy."

"I can see that," he said, studying her outfit.

"Were you able find out more about this Ghost guy?" Liam joined the conversation.

"No. To be honest, at this point I'm more than puzzled." Jerry scratched his head. He stopped and wrinkled his forehead. "However, I did receive a very interesting call from a man who lives on 5th Street. Said a British woman and a tall man asked to view his doorbell footage? You wouldn't happen to know something about that, would you?" Jerry exchanged a darting gaze with both of them.

This was not good, Isabella thought to herself, lowering her head and biting her lip. Liam stood next to her, placing a supporting hand on her shoulder.

"Do we need a lawyer?" he asked in a calm but unwelcoming voice.

Jerry threw his hands in the air before pulling out a chair to sit down. "Oh Jesus! Do you think I'd come here by myself waiting for an hour if you needed a lawyer?"

Liam seemed to think about it for a second, but then finally nodded. Isabella could feel her body relax, forcing out a deep breath.

"So, we are not in trouble?" Her gaze was focused in anticipation.

"If I thought that either of you were capable of murder or kidnapping, I wouldn't be sitting here in this weird, empty-looking apartment talking to the two of you."

Jerry could be a bit rough, but Isabella owed him a great deal. He was watching out for her, now more than ever.

"However…" His tone changed into a low voice that neither Isabella nor Liam liked. "I saw the footage of the video, and it's very serious. Especially since the red-haired woman had been reported missing since the day of the accident."

"What?" they both shouted.

Liam threw a hand to his head, nearly slapping it, while Isabella jerked back with her hands to her chest. They had been so busy, neither of them had really thought a great deal about what had happened to the woman in the footage. But then, neither of them really suspected that anything in fact did happen to the woman in the footage. Isabella's best guess was that she had run off in fear after she saw Isabella appear out of nowhere in a period dress.

"We have nothing to do with her kidnapping, or murder, or running away, or whatever it is," Liam said in a firm voice. His nostrils flared under glaring eyes.

Isabella, on the other hand, wasn't so sure about that any longer. Was it possible that she had something to do with this woman's disappearance? Was she the very reason for a life vanishing into thin air? She felt a chill creeping through her chest, making her sick to her stomach. Everything had changed once again, swinging the pendulum from a ray of sunshine to unpredictably worse. Stumbling over to the table, she managed to sit down next to Jerry just in time before her legs collapsed under her. Both men noticed her severe distress, staring at her as if they were waiting for her to speak.

Isabella shook her head in disbelief. "Who is she?" Her voice trembled.

"Her name is Emma Washington. She was a PhD student here at UPenn. She disappeared the night of your accident. Her mother filed a missing person report pretty much the next day."

Isabella was in shock. "This is all my fault." Her head crumpled onto her hand, smothering her face.

Liam rushed over to her, kneeling down to grab her hand. "No it's not. Don't say that. There's more to the story, isn't there Jerry?" He threw Jerry a piercing stare.

Jerry pressed his lips together in a show of respect. "I have to say, the military has trained you well in reading people."

Isabella frowned at Jerry, sending him a dazed look.

Jerry tried to compose himself. "Honestly, none of this makes any sense. I shouldn't even be telling you this. But then, I told you way too much already."

"What is it?" Isabella asked, finally finding her voice.

"Well..." Jerry started scratching his head again. "You see, this case is really quite unusual. Emma Washington no longer counts as a missing person, and yet she has never been found."

Isabella and Liam wrinkled their foreheads in confusion.

"I'm not a cop, but that doesn't make any sense," Liam said, gently stroking Isabella's hand with his thumb. Even under such terrible circumstances, his touch gave her a warm tingle in her stomach.

"And I'm a cop and it doesn't make sense to me either. All I know is that, about a week after Emma's mother filed a missing case report, she showed up with some crazy letter that was supposedly from Emma. It talked about starting over and not to worry about her any longer."

Relief struck Isabella as if she had been hit by lightning. This woman, Emma, she was still alive!

"What's so unusual about that?" Isabella asked inquisitively with hope written all over her face.

Jerry took a deep breath as if he needed strength for what he was about to say next. "I'll tell you what's so crazy about all of that. We had the letter tested and it came back as her handwriting…"
Thank God!

"So, she's okay then? If the letter came from her, then the case was solved, right?" Liam asked, struggling to make sense of all of this.

"Not at all. After confirming that it was indeed her letter, we found something else…" A deafening silence suffocated the empty room as Jerry wet his lips for what he was about to say next.

"The letter was dated from the late 1890s."

Isabella shot back to her feet, her eyes and mouth wide open. The chair she sat on almost fell over from the force of her abrupt motion. Liam stumbled backwards onto his butt, now seated on the floor. *Impossible! Impossible! Impossible!* The words kept ringing in her head like an alarm bell.

Jerry got up, inching his way toward her. "Isabella, are you all right?" His worry-filled voice tried to calm her down as he approached her, but before he could take another step, a sinister scratching coming from the other side of the apartment door instantly caught his attention.

Isabella's mind was in a frenzy while Liam jumped to his feet and stepped in front of her with a clenched fist, placing himself in between her and whatever threat was about to come. Jerry slowly drew his weapon, signaling them to keep quiet. Another ominous scratching assaulted the door, breaking the silence once more, followed by the door knob twisting and twitching and trembling from left to right.

Jerry walked up to the door, pointing his gun at whoever it was on the other side. Isabella clenched her jaw. The sound of her heartbeat was thrashing in her ears. She placed a hand on Liam's back to feel his warmth. Taking a peek from his side, she inched closer to him, pressing her body behind his. If this turned out to be her last moment, at least she had spent it with him. There couldn't have been a better end to her tragic life than at the side of the man who meant the world to her.

Jerry carefully placed a hand onto the door knob and turned to gesture a silent countdown toward Liam. Liam nodded, signaling back that he was ready.

"If things go bad, I will throw myself onto this guy and you run as fast and as far as you can. You hear me?" Liam whispered to her, but before Isabella got the chance to tell him that she would never just leave him behind, Jerry had already swung the door open, screaming at the top of his lungs.

"POLICE! ON THE GROUND! NOW!"

What followed next nobody could have expected in their wildest dreams. Appearing out from the shadow was a crinkly old face, long unkempt hair, thick ragged clothes, and a pair of broken glasses with big eyes peering over them.

"Stop waving that thing at me!" Dan angrily swatted the gun out of her face. She walked past Jerry and stopped in front of Liam. With mouths and eyes wide open, both men were frozen in shock. It took Isabella a moment to realize what was happening and get control over her body back, but she finally ran toward Dan with a big hug.

"Dan! I am so glad to see you!" She threw herself around Dan's neck. Dan turned her old

Denise Daye

frowning face into a grandmother's freshly baked smile, but then immediately put her famous poker face back on.

"All right, all right now, let's stop with this mushy horseshit," she said gently and let go of Isabella.

Jerry angrily slammed the door shut while Liam was still busy picking up his mouth off the floor.

"Are you out of your goddamn mind? I could have shot you!" he shouted at her, outraged.

Dan totally ignored him as if he was some disobedient grandchild and walked into Liam's kitchen, surveying the countertops for something.

"I agree. What the hell are you doing waving your gun around like a cowboy in the wild west?" she snickered.

Dan was now going through Liam's cabinets and took out a cup.

"She's exactly how I pictured her," Liam whispered into Isabella's ear.

Isabella crossed her arms with a grin. "You have no idea."

"What the hell are you doing here?" Jerry put his gun back into the holster.

"I'm here to warn Isabella about that little dark friend of hers." She filled the glass with tap water and took one big drink like it was a shot of tequila. "Phew...that's better. It took me three long damn hours to walk here."

Isabella gasped. "Did he hurt you?"

Dan calmly refilled the glass.

"We didn't get that far. The friend I stay at saw him lurking behind a light pole when she came back from work. By now that creep must know that you're no longer with me. So, I wanted to see for myself how hard you are to find." Her gaze shifted to Liam, scanning him from head to toe with laser-like eyes and snickered. "Turns out it's not hard at all."

Jerry now stepped closer. "So, you decided it's a good idea to lead him here? What if he followed you?" he barked at her.

"I've lived on the streets for decades. If I don't want to be followed, I'm not followed. Besides, I'm not the one parking a police car in front for the whole world to see," Dan said, crossing her arms.

Isabella studied her for a brief moment. She looked so different and yet so much the same under her raggedy clothes. Living with her friend had done Dan a lot of good. Her clothes may have been ragged, but they were the best looking ragged clothes you would ever see on Dan. Isabella remembered Jerry once telling her that Dan was one of the few homeless people who chose to live on the streets. Why, he didn't want to reveal. All he said was that it wasn't his story to tell.

As happy as she was seeing her good friend again, it brought just another set of bad news. It was almost as if her mother had placed a curse on her since birth, oiling the wheel of her misfortune to keep it spinning for eternity.

"So, it's only a matter of time now until he shows up." Liam peeked over the window. The side street was eerily empty.

Isabella sat back down, worn out of her mind. She felt her throat closing in and dropped her head into her hands, too exhausted to hold it up for another minute.

"Don't worry, I'll catch that creep," Jerry said in a comforting voice.

"About goddamn time you will," Dan replied. "I've been luring him down to the river park for the past few days now. He has no clue that I'm setting up a trap for him."

Jerry shook his head in anger. "That's great Dan, playing Navy CIS again? This isn't tv. This could be dangerous!" he reprimanded her.

"Couldn't we wait for him there?" Liam turned to Jerry.

"Am I speaking Chinese? Is anybody actually listening?" Jerry shook his head in disbelief.

Isabella ignored him as she had an idea of her own now. "What a great idea. I could go with Dan, so when he sees me—"

"Absolutely not!" Both men shouted.

Dan shook her head, glaring at them with protruding eyes. "Can we tone down the testosterone in here a bit?"

"Thank you, Dan," Isabella said, clearly irritated with both of them. She knew they meant well but couldn't help but feel that familiar feeling of being told what to do again. Her whole life she had been controlled by others, had been treated like a complete incompetent. Her life with Dan may have been rough, but at least she was her own woman. Isabella refused to go back into that golden cage—ever!

"I don't see the problem here. He obviously has no gun, and you'll be right there ready to arrest him."

For a moment, Liam was torn, incapable of reconciling the thought of having to protect her while at the same time accepting her right to put an end to all of this, even if she was placing herself in harm's way. It took a while, but Liam managed to press his lips together and give Isabella a silent nod that he got the hint. Jerry on the other hand saw things black and white with no grey zone in between. He crossed his arms and pushed his shoulders back.

"Let me tell you a few problems with this plan of yours... *A*, you're not a police officer. *B*, it's not safe. *C*, my guess is that it's more likely that he's the one setting the trap. And *D*, he might have a gun by now." He shook his head in a firm no. "But if you want, I can keep going all the way to *Z*."

"That won't be necessary," Isabella replied in a cold voice and turned toward Dan. "How can I get a hold of you? Do you have a cell phone now?"

Dan smirked and grabbed something from her pocket. "Even better, I have one for the both of us." She handed her the phone.

"Splendid."

Before Jerry or Liam could say another word, she continued in a determined tone that did not allow for further discussion.

"If you will excuse me now, I am awfully tired. This has been a very long day, hasn't it, Liam?"

Liam looked over to Jerry who clearly expected him to take his side, but much to his disappointment, Liam lended her a helping hand.

"Yes. It has been one of the most eventful days of my life. Let's continue this tomorrow."

Jerry let out a grumpy growl but didn't argue any further. "Fine. I'll stop by around five." He turned to open the front door. "You better be here tomorrow. And call 911 immediately when you see something. No hero stunts or John Wick stuff, you hear me?"

Isabella softened her mood, giving him a quick salute. "Loud and clear." But instead of leaving, he just stood there, lifting an eyebrow into the room, awaiting something.

Dan finally pouted back at him. "Yes, I guess it's about time to go."

"Well come on then, I'll drop you off. Unless you want to walk again for another three hours?" Dan glanced over to Isabella. The wrinkles that formed on her forehead told everything Isabella had to know.

"It's fine, Dan. I'll manage. We will talk again tomorrow."

"Fine. But call me if you need me." She joined Jerry as they both disappeared into the hallway and the door slammed shut.

Isabella and Liam stared at each other in silence across the empty room. For a while they didn't know what to say. It was a trying day filled with surprises and mixed emotions.

"I'm sorry about earlier. I didn't mean to sound overbearing." Liam broke the silence.

"No, I'm sorry. I know you're just concerned about me. It's just, my whole life people have controlled every aspect of my existence. What to eat, what to wear, what to say... Even who to marry. When I first woke up in this strange new world, I had nothing, but at least I was free to make my own decisions. It felt incredible, and I wish it would stay that way."

Liam nodded, lifting a hand to his chest, taking a step closer toward her. "I'm not trying to say I understand what it was like for you. It sounds awful. But I can—how do I say this—empathize. The military had my ass, literally, for a good part of my life. They could send me to war or have me clean toilets all day. In fact, they made me do both."

A feeling of shame washed over her. It made its way from her head down to her heart to leave a sharp pain. Not once had she taken the time to ask Liam how he was doing. It was more than obvious that he bore the scars of his own tale. But ever since she got here, everything had always been about her. She wanted to talk to him. Not about the weather or other unimportant things. She wanted to know him in a much deeper way. To feel the man who stood up for her. To reach down into his heart. To hear about his most memorable joys, as well as his greatest sorrows.

"Was it hard? Your time in the military?"

Liam pressed his lips together, drifting into thoughts.

"It was...," he said in barely more than a whisper.

A painful lump formed in her throat. Liam shook his head with an unfocused gaze and shallow sigh, tearing himself out of wherever his mind had just wandered off to. "No, not tonight. We sure have enough going on already. But if you want to, after all of this is over, I'll cook dinner for us and you can ask me whatever you want to know." He gave her a stare with eyes that seemed to be filled with pain—a brave soldier's burden. "I will answer truthfully." His faint smile touched her heart deeply.

When all of this is over, we might not get the chance to, she thought to herself, feeling the overbearing cold sadness that caved in her chest. But she wouldn't tell him that. "Yes, let's do that when all of this is over," she replied, veering off from his gaze. "I better rest now" were her last words before rushing behind the closed door.

Her throat choked in tears. Her legs finally gave in as she crumpled onto the floor. *After all of this is over...* She would be back in her own time. To be recognized as a noblewoman. Sleeping under golden sheets. Dining with dukes and princes of the time, and married off to some rich aristocrat, trapped in a golden cage. Of course, there was another option. She could continue defying her mother and dragging her brother along with her entire family into ruin. Whichever one it would be, it would be without Liam.

The church bell drowned out all the noise from outside. Isabella stood in front of the altar, wearing a wedding dress fit for a queen. A priest was holding an open bible in his hands, staring at her in great anticipation. She looked around and realized that the church was empty. The only person in attendance was her mother, who stood right behind her, almost as if she was holding her in place. Next to her was Lord Warrington wearing nothing but nappies. Without clothes to soak in his endless sweat, a stream of smelly fluids were running down his insufferable body, forming a puddle of putrid liquid underneath his feet. He giggled uncontrollably under half-missing dentures like a child.

Isabella tried to escape, but she couldn't. She was frozen in place. *Somebody help!* She tried to scream, but even her voice was empty. Lord Warrington turned toward her, grabbing her by the wrist so tightly that it hurt. He licked his lips as they turned into a perverted grin, ready for the part of the ceremony where he was supposed to kiss the bride. His whole face was wet with sweat. Isabella turned toward the only person in that place that could help her. *Mother, please!* But her mother just grinned from ear to ear with eyes that sparkled like she was staring at a chest filled with gold. Isabella fumbled to avoid their soulless gaze as her eyes scoured the room for help. But she found terror instead! In the far end of the church, hiding in the shadowy corner, was Ghost, staring at her in anticipation with the red eyes of an evil demon. Her body shook in horror. *Liam, help! Help me!* She tried to scream, to kick, to burst into tears, but bloody hell, she couldn't.

"HELP! LIAM! HELP ME!"

A loud bang assaulted the room as the door was violently swung open, waking her from her nightmare. She shot up in her bed, her fingers fumbled to grab the sheets to cover herself as little pearls of sweat ran down her forehead. She suddenly realized where she was; Liam was right next to her, putting a hand on her cheek.

"Are you ok?" His voice was in panic.

She was in disarray as she stared at him with her eyes wide open like an owl, breathing heavily.

"I... He tried to kiss me. I couldn't move. Then there was Ghost... Eyes like the devil."

Liam moved closer, sitting himself on the mattress next to her to pull her into his arms. "You are safe. It was just a nightmare." Giving her a gentle kiss on the forehead, he softly rocked her back and forth. "I won't let anybody hurt you."

She closed her eyes while he held her in his arms. His warm body was wrapped around hers.

She opened her eyes just enough to see him, only to notice that he was naked from his waist up, wearing nothing more than a pair of boxers. His bare chest was muscular, twitching, hard as steel.

Her desire flickered to life, sending heat waves down her spine. No man before Liam had ever been this close to her, and yet her body seemed to know exactly what she longed for. She was drunk with love. She slowly moved her head back, looking right at him. It was dark in the room but the light coming in from the window was enough to see a mixture of longing and uncertainty in his eyes. And before he could say another word, with her hands grasping at his thick shoulders, Isabella leaned forward and pressed her steaming lips onto his. Her heart skittered. His soft and warm lips opened to let out a moan.

"Isabella…"

Passion took a hold of her and Isabella's kisses became deeper, begging for his touch.

He suddenly pulled away just a few inches, breathing heavily, almost unable to speak. "Are you sure this is what you want…?"

She leaned in, softly stroking his lips with hers. "I never wanted anything this much in my life," she whispered, running her hand over his chest all the way down and into his boxers.

"Oh," she sighed in surprise, gently closing her hand around his big and hard steel. His eyes darkened and he grabbed her wrist.

"This isn't a game, Isabella," he growled in arousal.

"I couldn't agree more," she moaned back at him, softly moving her hand up and down his manhood. His eyes flickered in a way she had never seen before as he pushed her with his body onto the mattress, locking her in place in between his legs.

"Isabella," he moaned, gently kissing the side of her neck, moving his lips down all the way to her breasts. He pulled up her shirt and took one of her peaks into his mouth, gently sucking on it.

"Oh my." She let out a sharp sound of pleasure.

Liam softly continued his trail of kisses all the way down to her pajama pants. "If you don't stop me, I will kiss you everywhere," he whispered under heavy breath.

But Isabella lifted up her hips to make it easier for him to pull down her pajama pants and underwear all the way until she was completely naked.

"I have dreamt of tasting you so many times," he moaned in between her legs, slowly running his lips up the inside of her thighs.

Despite her innocence, she knew where he was headed. Her body trembled in response, begging for him to continue. But right before he reached her longing core of pleasure, he paused, waiting for her gaze to meet his. Before she could beg him to do as he pleased, he slowly descended his soft lips into her most intimate part, closing his eyes in pure pleasure. A fire rushed through her veins, causing her shudders of delight. She could feel his tongue gently licking her, robbing her of her ability to breathe.

"You taste so good…," he growled against her burning cave.

Her nails buried deep into the mattress beneath her. She didn't know what it was that was pushing her harder and harder, but much to her relief, it only took a few more of Liam's skillful kisses to push her over that edge her center was seeking. Every muscle in her body tensed as she let out a loud, sensual scream before collapsing underneath him. Liam gave her one last tender kiss before he pulled his face away from her center to position himself on top of her, softly kissing her again on her lips.

"We are just getting started, my love." She moaned playfully as he dragged her lower lip with his teeth. Instantly, her body started tingling and aching for his touch again. She could feel his pulsating length right where his tongue had been pleasuring her moments ago. Her body trembled in response, and before he could lower himself to slowly slip inside her, she grabbed him by his buttocks with both of her hands and pulled him down into her, sliding his manhood right where she knew it belonged.

Liam let out a loud growl, but instead of pleasure for Isabella, she could feel a sharp stabbing pain right where he entered her. Isabella shut her eyes, throwing her head to the side, hoping for the burning to subside. Liam instantly pushed himself up onto his elbows, looking down onto her in shock. He shook his head in disbelief.

"You are a virgin?" He was staring at her, waiting for her gaze to meet his. When it finally did, she could see the distress in his eyes. She had to do something right now or he would pull away from her. She began rotating her hips while making deep and prolonged eye contact with him. The pain she felt at first disappeared and she could feel him grow harder and larger inside her.

"Isabella don't…," he moaned in protest, but she held him close, moving faster and faster.

"I want you…," she said, out of breath.

He pressed his lips against hers. "Babe, please stop… I won't last much longer…," he said, kissing her passionately.

And just as he said those words, he let out a growling scream and at the same time she could feel a warm liquid pulsate into her. Her whole body tingled. He was gasping for air, his brows closely drawn together, before finally collapsing onto her. For a moment they just lay there, not moving, listening to each other's hearts hammering against their chests. Isabella had never been happier before than in this very moment. *I love you*, she said to him in her thoughts.

Liam looked down onto Isabella. She looked so incredibly beautiful. Never had he felt such an intense connection with anybody else. He didn't even know it could feel like this. And under any other circumstances, he would stay inside her, keep kissing her again until both of their sparks turned into flames of lust again. But it wasn't any other circumstance — he had just taken her virginity.

"Oh stop looking at me like that," she said, pushing him off her to be able to reach for her pajama pants.

Liam pulled his boxers back up as well. For a moment he didn't know what to say. He shouldn't feel bad. She wanted this as much as he did, but he still felt awful. If any of those historical movies he had seen were even in the slightest accurate, Isabella was now considered ruined. Not in his world, but back in her own time where women were considered a man's property. Had she even considered that? Or would she now realize what they had done and break out in tears of regret?

"I just feel awful about this. I really do. I came in here because I heard you scream. I was in no way planning this." He tried to read her facial expression, but she was giving him her famous Victorian lady poker face. She sat up and put her hair into a bun.

"Aren't you supposed to hold me all night rather than feeling regret? At least that is what would happen in those twenty-first century moving pictures of yours," she said with a sarcastic grin. He sat up as well, rubbing his neck.

"Yes, but those moving pictures usually don't focus on a man ruining a woman who has to time travel back into her own world where she might be considered an outcast for much less than what we just did."

She put her hand onto his shoulder. "Liam, I wanted this."

He leaned his cheek onto her hand. "That doesn't make it right on my end."

All of a sudden, she pulled away. Was that anger he saw in her eyes?

"Out of all the people... How can you treat me like a little girl that has no say over her own life?"

He grabbed her hand and held it to his chest. "That's not what I meant." She pulled away again, standing up.

"No, that is exactly what you meant. Isabella Astley. People in her own world oppress her for *their* own sake, and people in this world oppress her for *her* own sake." She was clearly angry at him now. He stood up as well, trying to calm her.

"I really didn't mean it like that when I—"

"Why is it that no matter where or *when* I go, people try to tell me what I can and cannot do?" She started pacing up and down the room. This was not going well for him.

"I am not trying to control you, I—"

She didn't listen to him. "I can't even give myself to a man without being told if that's right or wrong, so how is that not…" She didn't get to finish her sentence as Liam grabbed her by her wrist and pulled her in his arms.

"I care for you so much it's ridiculous," he said in a soft voice, sinking his lips onto hers. Without the slightest protest, she kissed him back, all the anger gone, as if that was all it took — a kiss. He gently lifted up her chin to make her look into his eyes. "I don't want to control you. I just want what's best for you because you mean a lot to me." Suddenly, a painful knot formed in his throat. Looking deep into these beautiful eyes, he couldn't think of anything else but that they would sooner or later look at another man, a man dressed in fancy clothes living in a golden castle in Victorian England. Isabella must have had similar sad thoughts. Biting her lower lip, tears formed in her eyes. It instantly made him feel worse. She kissed him again.

"I care for you too. A lot." Her tears were now rolling down her cheeks, dropping onto his bare chest. He didn't have to ask why she was crying. He felt close to tears himself. They deeply cared for each other, there was no doubt. But that didn't change the fact that she did not belong in this world—nor belong to him. Their time together was limited, and if his sister was as smart—or as crazy—as he knew she was, tomorrow would be the very day they would find out when and how their tragic love story would come to an end.

CHAPTER 13

Isabella opened her eyes and rolled onto Liam's side of the bed. It still felt warm, but he was no longer there. She closed her eyes for a moment, her mind replaying last night. Butterflies swirled through her stomach as she thought about their tender moments. It was as if she were floating on air. But there was also a deep sadness that came along with it. For the first time in her life she'd found love, and was loved. She was finally happy. But like so many times before, life did not bless her with love but rather cursed it. Nothing but an illusion under borrowed time. None of it was supposed to happen. Not in the twenty-first century. Not with Liam. Not in 1881. Not ever.

Isabella got dressed and walked into the kitchen. Liam did not have breakfast prepared like the day before. But he did have coffee ready. He was pouring himself a cup when he noticed her with a smile.

"Good morning." He walked over, leaning in to give her a soft kiss on the lips.

"Good morning." Isabella blushed, hidden under her smile. He did an excellent job pretending nothing was the matter. Isabella decided it would be best to do the same. At this point there wasn't much either of them could do about the whole situation. She had to go back, for her brother; or otherwise despise herself for the rest of her life.

"I'm afraid there's no time for my world-famous pancakes. We have to head out to Eva's house." Isabella surveyed the room for a clock but then remembered that people in the twenty-first century mostly relied on their phones now. "What time is it?"

"It's 9:40."

"9:40! Are you sure?" Isabella was awoken for the second time.

"Mm-hmm…" He nodded, grabbing his shoes out from the entrance hall. That was incredible. She had never slept that long. It was considered improper for a lady to do so. As ridiculous as this sounded, it felt liberating to sleep in.

"We'll get something on the way so we don't have to eat at my sister's house. Only God knows what hides in the depths of that woman's fridge."

Isabella laughed, exasperated as she remembered the bug-flavored cookies his sister had given them.

"Does that mean no ladybug toast for breakfast?"

Liam flinched, shaking the memory from his head in disgust. "I will take you to something equally disgusting. Something more American than cowboy boots."

Isabella took another big bite of the round sandwich which she held with both hands. Her eyes twinkled like her soul had just been rejuvenated. Liam threw her a grin, keeping his gaze on the road.

"This is the most incredible food I have ever tasted!"

She grabbed another onion ring and dipped it in the small rectangular plastic container with the sauce that was called honey-mustard. "I mean it. This is better than the Queen's Christmas dinner! This man is truly a king."

Liam burst into laughter. "I don't think Burger King has anything to do with gourmet food or royalty. Quite the opposite."

Isabella gave him a quick angry look and spoke with a high chin. "Well, to me he is. I recognize him as such. This food is *the real deal*, as you Americans would say."

Liam laughed even harder. "You can call me king too if you like. My pancakes are pretty amazing."

"That's what I thought too," she said, quickly raising a finger into the air. "But that was before I had a taste of the King's."

She took another big bite. Liam grabbed the empty paper bags and pushed them under his car seat.

"We better not let Eva see this, otherwise we will be hearing about it until the end of time." A baffled Isabella hid hers under her seat as well. Eva was truly unusual in a brilliant way. Never had she come across a smarter and sassier person than her. Isabella liked her a lot, with the exception of her choice of food.

Liam pulled up in front of Eva's house. Much to their surprise, she had been waiting for them outside. She was dressed all in white, from jacket to shoes, with her arms crossed and chin up, staring down at them. Her hair stood out, put up in a bun, tied together with a rainbow colored string. Liam pulled the car window down to lean outside.

"Are we going somewhere?" he asked.

"Of course we are. Why else would I be standing out here waiting for you. By the way, you're late." She opened the door at the back and got in.

"Two minutes." Liam snickered, avoiding eye contact.

"As I said… Late." She typed something into her phone and handed it to Liam. "Here, follow these directions."

He stared on the screen for a second, wrinkling his forehead. "Is this a joke?" He turned to face Eva.

"Why would it be?" She rolled her eyes at him.

He started to read the directions out loud. "Follow the highway north until you see a happy redwood tree. Turn right. Follow that road until you see the sad Swamp Saloon. Don't have a drink. Turn right again on the dirt road behind their parking lot. Once you lose your cell signal, drive ten more minutes and you will find me."

It was silent in the car for a second. Isabella was on her tippy toes pressed hard on the car mat trying hard not to laugh. Eva crossed her arms yet again.

"I already told you you'd have to have an open mind. Mama doesn't like technology, so you can't find her with Google maps."

"Mama?" Liam stared at her, leaning back with one eyebrow raised and the other pulled down. Eva lifted her chin in defiance.

"Listen, we can either do this or call it off and I can go back inside and finish my thesis on wave-particle duality. Your call."

Liam looked over to Isabella who didn't have to say *please*. It was written all over her face. Liam took a deep breath.

"Fine, but this Mama better not be some Blair Witch type of fellow."

Isabella placed a hand on his arm with a grateful, faint smile. Liam put the car in reverse, pulling it back toward the road when Eva pulled something out from underneath his seat.

"Karma, have mercy on his aura! Please tell me you didn't poison poor Isabella with this garbage!"

Liam took a quick glance at his sister from the rearview mirror and saw her holding up the crumpled bag from Burger King. He let out a long, slow sigh and clenched his fists around the steering wheel.

"Lord, if you hear me, please have mercy on us... This is gonna be a long ride," he whispered just loud enough for Isabella to hear as they made their way toward Neverland.

"This is exactly how horror movies start," Liam said sarcastically looking up to the thick clouds that had magically appeared the moment they pulled onto this dirt road, turning a sunny sky into a dark-grey overcast one within minutes. It was eerily cold in this part of the woods, or wherever they were at the moment. Tall trees buried under deep fog surrounded them, forming walls that seemed to be closing in on them the farther they went, ready to swallow them whole.

It was a miracle but two hours and several wrong turns later, they finally made it to the dirt road behind the Swamp Saloon.

"This isn't as scary as the garbage you eat," Eva countered his earlier remarks. Isabella had no idea that Liam wasn't joking when he'd tried to hide those paper bags, warning about his sister's lengthy speeches.

"Eva... Please! In case this lady kills us, I don't want to die listening to you preach about fair-trade food." Liam bared his teeth, one word away from bursting into anger or perhaps tears.

Isabella giggled, watching all of this with a fuzzy feeling in her heart. "You guys are really lucky to have each other," she said with a grin.

Neither Liam nor Eva replied to that, but their silence was a sign that they agreed with her.

The car pulled into an opening in the woods which was the end of the road. There was a big, green house that looked like it was built in Victorian times. It was asymmetrical with round towers that had steep pitched roofs. A large wraparound porch would have given it a cozy touch if it weren't for the visible dry rot in several places. Ravens nestled high up on the roof, watching them in silence as they got out of the car.

Isabella felt her muscles tighten. "It looks like a doll's house," she said, trying to lift her spirits.

Liam wrinkled his nose. "More like a haunted house."

"Don't be ridiculous. Mama hasn't done any dark magic in months," Eva barked at him as if it was the most normal thing in the world.

"Well, I am glad to hear that Mama found her way back to the light," Liam said, rolling his eyes.

Isabella threw Liam a look with a mix of worry and confusion.

He grabbed her hand, repenting his words. "Don't worry, this is all a bunch of b.s. if you ask me."

They were making their way up the porch when the front door slowly squeaked open. Isabella took a step behind Liam. All three stood there staring into the dark hallway that was soon touched by the dim sunlight hiding behind the clouds. The walls inside were filled to the brim, from antique books and furniture, to pictures and more bizarre unidentifiable stuff, all of which seemed to be fighting for more wall space.

"Mama?" Eva's voice echoed across the hallway and back. "Are you there?"

She took the first step inside the darkly lit corridor. But there was no answer. Eva turned to Liam and Isabella, who still stood in the safety of the dim sunlight shrugging their shoulders as if they were ready to go back home.

"Eva!" a voice shrieked from behind them, causing all three of them to be startled and alarmed.

"Jesus Christ." Liam let out a sharp breath.

Isabella threw her arm around his shoulder, pulling herself closer to his back. Even Eva had a hand lifted to her mouth, but instantly lowered it, playing it cool again.

Mama revealed herself as a short, white-haired woman who wore what looked like an old medieval, green wool garment. She stood in front of Liam and Isabella and from the look on her face, she'd just come from the woods and had leaves still stuck to her hair. She was carrying a bundle of sticks on one arm and a basket on the other filled with different odd-looking leaves.

"Ah. Thank goodness you're here. I thought I wouldn't make it one more step!" she said out of breath with a raspy voice, pushing the branches and the basket into Liam's arms. Without saying another word, she pushed past Eva and faded into the house. The three of them stared at each other, then followed her through the dark entrance and into another darkly lit room. Everything in this home looked like it was out of an old-period horror movie. Old pictures of a century long gone heavily decorated the walls. The furniture was as old, if not older, than Mama herself. Liam almost tripped over a rug, but Isabella managed to hold onto him, just barely avoiding a fall on a rusty spike-filled mace just lying on the floor. To its right stood a full-size knight's armor with an empty hand.

"Would you mind if I turn a lamp on?" Liam asked, catching his breath, slightly annoyed.

"I don't have electricity," Mama said. She kindled several candles, then pointed to a table pushed against the wall next to an old piano, signaling Liam to put the branches and the basket on top.

"You don't have electricity?" he asked in disbelief, following her orders and putting her voodoo witchcraft items down. Mama threw him a long annoyed stare.

"I could see if I could get that installed for you," he clarified his intentions. "It looks a bit dangerous using candles with so much wood around."

Mama's facial expression changed from annoyed and angry to a kinder version of annoyed. "Thank you, but I can manage. All these new world wonders interfere with the flow of my energy."

"Right…" Liam scratched his head.

"Thanks for helping us." Eva stepped closer to Mama.

Mama locked her gaze onto Isabella, which for some reason sent shivers down her spine.

"Of course. You were very kind to me back then, Eva. I owe you this much." Mama nodded toward a red satin sofa. "Have a seat, I'll be right back."

Isabella sat down first, unleashing a cloud of dust bursting into the air that instantly swallowed all three of them. Isabella let out a feminine cough, while Liam and Eva sounded like they had bronchitis, with red eyes welling in tears.

Cough. "From where—" *Cough* "...do you know this lady?" Liam demanded answers.

"I helped her win a court case—" *Cough.* "She didn't want to be listed..." *Cough.* "On Google Maps."

Both of them waited for the dust to settle before sitting back down next to Isabella.

"Are we supposed to all hold hands?" Liam asked with a smirk.

"Don't be ridiculous." Eva rolled her eyes.

"I'm not the one who is ridiculous," he mumbled, nodding at everything around them.

Mama came back with some sort of incense burning in her hand. Without saying another word, she walked straight to Isabella who stared at her yellowish face glowing from the candle light with curious wide eyes.

"So, you are the one who does not belong here." Mama spoke like she was summoning a ghost on a Ouija board. Isabella glanced at Liam, who was studying Mama with an expression on his face that was hard to read.

"Well go on, child, don't be shy. Mama has seen and heard more than you could imagine." She was now speaking like a shaman, carefully flapping the incense in a wide circle in front of Isabella. Liam nodded at Isabella as she thought of what to say.

"I guess you could say that." She chose her words carefully. On the drive here, Liam had advised her to give as little information to Mama as possible. He explained that people like Mama, who think they have special *gifts*, would gather information provided to them and spit them back out in a form of some prophecy that sounded like they knew things nobody else could, but the truth was more or less just an educated guess.

"Do you have anything you brought with you on this journey?" Isabella pulled out her coin which glistened under the glow of the warm little fires around them.

"Yes, this coin." She handed it over.

Mama analyzed the cryptic item in her wrinkly old fingers, then clenched her fist tightly around it, closing her eyes shut. For a moment she just stood there, being carefully watched by three curious pairs of eyes. But then all of a sudden she started singing, wiggling her bum in rhythm with the burning incense up and down, round and round, howling loudly like a Viking war cry ready for Valhalla as she danced in circles.

Liam was the first to find the voice to say something.

"Are you kidding me?" He rubbed his eyes in exhaustion, accompanied by a loudly howling Mama.

An overwhelming sadness rippled into Isabella's heart. The feeling of disappointment hit her like a train at full speed, grinding away every bit of hope she had left inside. This was supposed to help her back home, make sense of it all. Her time travel, her life. But instead she was sitting in a dusty old house, cut off from the rest of the world, listening to a human imitating animal cries.

Liam looked over and noticed her eyes gazing down to the ground, lost to the moment. He stood up, jaw clenched in anger as he tried to pull her away to protect her from all of this nonsense.

"Let's go, this was a waste of time!"

Isabella gave Mama a final look of hope. Mama rolled her eyes back and screamed even louder, making noises that didn't sound like any animal known to mankind, accompanied by overly exaggerated movement.

"I agree, let us go…" Isabella closed her fingers around Liam's hand. But just when Isabella was ready to get up and leave, Mama leaped toward her, falling onto her knees. She held up the coin in a tightly trembling clenched fist with both eyes pinched shut, and finally spoke in a language they all found familiar.

"I see a duchess whose treasure box is always empty," she growled in a low voice.

Isabella was now gripping onto Liam's hand, pulling him back in place to stop him from leaving. It was utterly impossible!

"My mother…," Isabella whispered, barely able to breathe.

"Green… I see an evergreen forest swallowing a black well." Mama now suddenly and violently swung her head to the side. "No! Not forest… A woman. Red hair. She took your place. You took hers. Wishes made from melted hearts…"

Isabella felt her chest tightening while her quivering hand grasped her wide-open mouth. Even Liam couldn't help but stand still in place like a statue. Eva, on the other hand, was watching the whole thing totally relaxed, even leaning an arm on the couch. As impossible as this seemed, Mama's *gift* was as real as the sun that was hiding behind the clouds.

"How do I get back!" Isabella found her voice, stumbling a few steps toward Mama. "My brother, is he all right?" she added hastily.

Mama fell forward, her whole body now shaking uncontrollably. "Pain... I see pain. And suffering... I am losing them..."

"No!" Isabella wailed in despair, falling onto her knees right in front of Mama. "Is he in pain? How can I get back?"

Mama trembled in silence. Isabella grabbed her shoulder, desperate to get the answer she needed. "How do I return?" she cried out, but Mama didn't answer. Isabella now turned to Liam who was right next to her, her big wet eyes begging for help. At first, he didn't seem to know how, but then kneeled down next to her.

"How does she get back home?" he almost begged into Mama's ear, to no effect.

All of a sudden, Mama grabbed Isabella by the wrist. Her grip was so strong and powerful that it hurt. She raised her head up and looked right into Isabella's eyes as if her burning gaze could see her every past, present, and future seeking the answers to her questions.

"Ghost…," she whispered. "The Ghost has the answers…" Those were Mama's last words before letting go of her and crumbling onto the floor, briefly unconscious. Liam held onto Mama, carefully trying to help her back up. "Are you ok?"

But Mama didn't answer. Eva rushed over next to them.

"Liam, lay her onto her back." He grabbed Mama under her arms to pull her flat onto the floor. Isabella grabbed a pillow from the couch and placed it under her head.

"She just needs a minute. Crossing dimensions is very tiring," Eva said, holding Mama's hand.

Liam fell backwards onto his butt, letting out the air that had been trapped since the entire thing started. "This is insane. All of this," he said shaking his head.

"I know," Eva put a hand on his shoulder. "There are many things that we don't understand about this world, even though humanity has been claiming to do so for countless years." She snickered.

"Indeed." Isabella agreed, nodding her head, then shaking it, then nodding once more.

Mama finally opened her eyes and turned her head toward Isabella.

"The night you came here, do you remember the words of your heart?" she whispered out of breath.

Isabella looked confused. "I'm not certain I understand."

Mama gently placed her wrinkly old hand on hers. "Close your eyes, child," Mama softly instructed her.

"Your heart... Try to listen to your heart..."

Isabella closed her eyes. A rush of memories came flooding into her mind and sinking into her thoughts, until one memory outpaced them all. The dreadful evening at the opera came back to her, all the way toward the hurtful things her mother said, and the coin that she threw at her.

"Your heart, listen to it..." Mama's voice pierced into her soul, and right there and then she felt it. A painful sting of loneliness and despair eating her inside. At first she thought it was a feeling of lost hope, but when she saw herself bending over to pick up the coin, she felt it as clear as the sun shining through the forest with its light piercing through the canopy, illuminating a single wild flower on the musky, grass-littered floor.

"A wish," Isabella's voice trembled, a tear rolling down her cheek, "to be someone else. To be loved and cherished… To be far, far away."

Isabella's eyes carefully opened to see Liam, Eva, and Mama gaze upon her in sadness. The burning sensation in her heart had come out in the form of tears as she tried to shake off those horrible feelings of solitude and hopelessness which she had felt that very night. Liam moved closer to take her in his arms.

"I didn't want to be me anymore. I wanted to be gone, happy, away, loved," she said, fighting against the tears. Liam held her close, leaning his head onto hers.

"But how is this wish connected to her being here?" Eva turned to Mama.

"The other woman, the red-haired one. She must have had the same wish, at precisely the exact same time, doing the exact same thing."

"You mean bending over and getting hit by a car?" Liam asked.

"Or carriage," Isabella answered.

With Eva's help, Mama got back on her feet. She looked depleted.

"Nobody really knows what forces are at play when it comes to life." Mama massaged her aching neck.

"So how do I return?" Isabella sounded calmer under Liam's comforting hug.

"I don't know. I really don't." Mama rubbed her eyes.

"We should let you rest then," Eva said.

"Yes, of course," Isabella agreed, taking Liam's hand to pull her back up. She walked over to Mama to grab her hand. "Thank you, Mama. With all my heart."

Mama nodded as they began to walk out. They were already outside, walking down the crumbling old porch, when Mama shouted from behind. "Don't forget... The Ghost has the answers."

Liam and Isabella froze and exchanged worried looks. Eva frowned at their reaction; she was clearly not in the loop. "Ghost? Do you know what she is talking about?"

Isabella bit her lower lip. "I am afraid so."

Liam took a deep breath in and forced the air back out in a sharp, determined manner. "It's rather complicated."

Inside the car, Liam brought the engine to life. He stared at Isabella who was staring right back at him as he gave her a reaffirming nod.

"Let's get some answers from that bastard," he said, cracking his knuckles.

CHAPTER 14

After dropping Eva off at her house, Isabella and Liam were jolted back into the present by the sight of Jerry waiting with Dan in front of Liam's apartment. He seemed to be in a good mood despite spending the last few hours with Dan who happened to be a master in pushing people's buttons.

Thanks to Dan's phone, Isabella had already texted her to be as agreeable as possible at this visit, not questioning any of her remarks to Jerry. Much to her surprise, Dan did a marvelous job of helping Isabella convince Jerry that Ghost was all his to take into custody. Two hours later, Jerry was finally convinced, or most probably exhausted at this point arguing with Dan, and headed back to the station.

Isabella leaned against the door, looking up to the ceiling from where Jerry had just disappeared. She felt horrible lying to him, but she had no choice.

"So why are we putting on this Oscar-worthy performance?" Dan asked, wiping some stains off her half-broken glasses.

"Because we are going to set a trap for Ghost," Isabella answered as she sat down at the table next to Liam. Dan didn't turn around, too preoccupied with rummaging through Liam's fridge. She found a plate with yesterday's pancakes that were half eaten. The smiley face was now missing an eye and half of its whipped cream grin. She turned to Liam with a suspicious stare, debating in her mind whether or not it was edible and why food had to have a face. Does he enjoy eating food with faces?

"It's a man-cake," he said proudly.

"Mm-hmm..." Dan snickered, closing the fridge, signaling that she had made her choice. She didn't bother to get a fork and came straight over to the table.

"I am on board with whatever you plan to do with that daemon, but why not get Jerry involved? I know he can be a bit annoying, but the man does have a gun and the license to shoot it."

She stopped next to Liam, close enough to invade his personal space. Liam got the hint and gave her his seat. He would have done so anyway, which made Isabella smile watching the whole scene.

"We can't have the police involved," Liam said, picking up Rambo who was rubbing himself against his leg, demanding attention.

"And why not?" Dan asked, holding the pancake like it was a hamburger and starting to devour it.

"Because we need answers. Answers we could never get once the police have him locked up." Liam gave in to Rambo's demands by scratching him under his chin. Isabella followed his moves, thinking to herself that this man looked even sexier while petting a cat.

"What kind of answers?" Neither Isabella nor Liam answered.

"Oh please, I already know that you're not from here... Not Philly, not America, not even this world," Dan said as if it they were having small talk about the weather.

For some reason, Isabella wasn't surprised at all. She had gotten used to her every single oddness. To be honest, Isabella missed most of it, but she still threw Liam a quick look. He shrugged his shoulders as if telling her *it's up to you, but I don't see why not.*

"You're too smart for this world," Isabella said, nodding at her.

Dan took the last bite of the pancake. "Not smart—I'm not blind. You have a glow in you that has long been lost in this world."

Things could not have gone any better. She didn't even have to go into all the details with Dan.

"You are truly amazing, Dan." Isabella put her hand on Dan's arm. She meant it from the bottom of her heart. Dan was one of the most amazing people she had ever come across, besides Liam, that was.

"Mm-hmm…," Dan mumbled, catching Liam's gaze, directing it toward her oily hands to signal him that she needed a paper towel. Liam rolled his eyes and left, then came back with a pair of napkins that he handed to Dan.

"So, any ideas yet how to set up that trap for this so-called Ghost?"

"Yes." Isabella spoke before Liam could even give it a thought. "We wait until it's dark. For whatever reason, he feels safe in the shadows. Then you will have him follow you from your place to the river again. Do you think you could make him stalk you?"

"That jokester is following me wherever I go as soon as it gets dark. He never gets close enough, but I know he's there. I usually get rid of him near the church. No one follows Dan if she doesn't want to be followed," Dan said with a high chin.

"Splendid! Then I guess it's settled." Isabella seemed to shine.

"Didn't you say he won't show himself if he sees me?" Liam asked, placing Rambo on his shoulder.

"Well…" Isabella pursed her lip and swallowed the lump in her throat, debating in her head whether to tell him now or later, knowing this one would not sit well with him. "That is why you won't be—"

"Absolutely not!" Liam waved his hand like he was slashing the air in his way. Rambo immediately jumped off, running toward the bedroom.

"That is way too dangerous!" His harsh voice and flaring nostrils did not allow any room for replies.

"Just hear me out." Isabella edged closer toward him, refusing to back down. "This Ghost is way too smart. He will see you before you even notice him. Then we will never be able to confront him."

"There is some truth in that," Dan joined in, breaking up the tension. "This Ghost no longer shows himself to groups of people. He's adapted, showing himself only to his target, like a real ghost." Dan leaned back in her chair. "Sometimes I wonder if he really is one." She snorted.

"If he shows himself in front of Dan, he might not be bothered by me either?" Liam countered.

"Sorry to shatter your rosy world views, but people don't really hold the homeless in high regards. He wouldn't think of me as much of a threat. He already tried to attack me once, and I still have a bone to pick with that bastard. Besides, I'm the best chance he has in finding her."

Isabella nodded in agreement. "Thank you, Dan. We have to approach this with logic not brute force." She crossed her arms, thinking that Dan was on her side.

"However…" Dan continued much to Isabella's displeasure. "I agree with army boy here. It's too dangerous without him. I won't put you at risk like that."

Isabella tilted her head with a downturned mouth. If those two thought they could just hide her like the spoiled, entitled child she used to be, they were wrong. She drew her brows together, arms stiff and steady, bracing for impact and ready for battle when Dan threw her off course.

"Did I ever tell you how I became homeless?"

This was so unexpected, Isabella couldn't get a word out. "Good to know that Jerry can keep his mouth shut. Anyway..." Dan's eyes turned dull, staring out toward the window. Her shoulders slumped and her eyes seemed like she was about to cry, but she didn't. Her posture changed from a feisty old woman to someone broken.

"I was married once," Dan said in a monotone voice and stopped for a brief moment like time itself ceased around her. Isabella had never seen Dan like this before.

"My husband. I loved him dearly. He was my rock, you know." A faint smile crossed her lips as her mind wandered off in thought.

"What happened?" Isabella asked, feeling a tight sensation choking her up from the inside, hurting her in the deepest corners of her heart.

"He died," Dan said crossing her arms, holding onto her shoulders. "It was his birthday. We had friends come over for dinner, and I sent him out to get us a bottle of expensive wine. We already had wine at home, but it wasn't good enough for me.

We argued about it. He said who cares if it's not fancy? Stubborn as I am, I wouldn't let it go until I won the argument. So he went to buy one. It was the last time I ever saw him. His car was T-boned by a construction truck and he died on impact."

"Oh Dan!" Isabella threw herself on Dan, covering her in a tight hug with tears streaming down her face. "I'm so terribly sorry."

For a while, Dan was motionless and out of place before finally leaning her head back, staring at the ceiling as if she were swallowing her tears and forcing them to flow back into her eyes.

"It's all good now. I blamed myself for a long time. Wanted nothing to do with the insurance money. I just wanted to be left alone. The streets felt like a fitting place for me."

"It wasn't your fault," Liam said with a warm, sad smile.

Dan looked at him under Isabella's tight hug. "No, but I shall carry my punishment till my last breath. And don't try to convince me otherwise." She placed a hand on Isabella and gave her arm a gentle squeeze, clearly appreciating the gesture of comforting her. "Thank you." Dan leaned back into her chair as she felt Isabella's warm touch on top of her wrinkly old hand.

"The reason why I told you this isn't to make us all go on an emotional rollercoaster ride. I'm telling you this because I couldn't take it if something ever happened to you. I would blame myself forever, just like I blamed myself for what happened to my husband. It would be more than I could bear." Both their eyes met in a deep meaningful gaze, staring at each other's soul, seeing into each other's hearts, knowing they were not much different after all. Dan held out a hand to wipe Isabella's tears away. Isabella nodded to show Dan that she understood and would respect her wish.

"So if I can't be the bait, what else could we do? He won't come close enough for you to catch him unless he sees me." Liam started walking up and down, stroking his chin, stuck deep in thought. Then suddenly he stopped with a face that looked as if he'd just figured it all out. He smiled with that handsome, cheeky smile of his that made him look irresistible.

"Thinks he sees you…" Dan and Isabella exchanged confused looks.

"What do you mean?"

Liam took huge strides like he just leaped toward the table they sat on. He placed both hands on it, almost slamming them in place while leaning closer toward them. "Do you still have that beautiful but totally wrong century dress of yours?"

Isabella could not be more confused. Dan on the other hand started to grin.

"Yes. It's in that plastic bag in the bedroom. Why?"

Liam enthusiastically pushed himself back up from the table with a huge grin stuck to his face. "Because the answer to this problem lies in the most unmanly thing I have ever done."

Dan met his gaze. "More unmanly than those man-cakes?"

"That's not for me to decide." He stared at Isabella with a suspicious-looking smile.

Isabella tried to stay as serious as she could, but her chest ultimately gave in and she burst out into laughter that sounded more like she was trying to gasp for air. Never had she had the pleasure of seeing a man dressed like this. Liam had finally revealed himself after disappearing into the bedroom for quite some time, and much to her surprise, he was wearing her dress!

He only wore the outer dress, most likely due to the fact that there was absolutely no way for the undergarments to fit his muscular frame. The dress hung loosely over his defined shoulders and was too short, revealing his ankles and feet. Isabella clapped as if she had just witnessed the most marvelous opera performance, screaming *bravo*.

"You look breathtaking!" she said, still laughing and out of breath.

"Definitely worse than the man-cakes." Dan shook her head in disbelief.

"Thank you, both of you," Liam said with a fierce grin, strutting his stuff like he was a supermodel on a runway. "I am confident enough of a man to not let you question my manhood."

"Ghost will never fall for this. You'll scare the man to death, maybe even have the police on our tail thinking you're some kind of pervert." Dan covered her forehead with one of her hands. "I can already hear the radios going, 'A huge pervert in a period dress is running loose on the streets of Philly, shoot on sight.'" Dan tried not to laugh at her own joke.

Liam was unfazed. "That's because the magic happens in the dark," he said in a sexy voice, throwing Isabella a wink that made her blush in laughter.

"He's definitely getting himself shot." Dan rolled her eyes toward Isabella.

Liam walked over to the light switch and turned it off. The room fell into darkness with just enough light coming in from the window to form his silhouette. "How about now?"

Isabella and Dan stared at him in utter astonishment. The shadows of the night had transformed a muscular, tall man in an overly small dress into a true Victorian lady. Isabella's dress was just fluffy enough to hide Liam's manly figure—if you were half blind that is or it was dark.

"I have to say, I am rather impressed!" Isabella tried to be serious, just inches away from having her chest explode into laughter. "From several meters away, I think you could pass for a true lady!"

"Yeah. If he was a mile away and the other person had worse eyesight than mine." Dan smirked. But then she stood up to get a better look at Liam. "But seeing that we are out of options, I think this might actually work," she agreed.

"Good." Liam gave Dan a thumbs-up before turning the lights back on. "Now. Let's work on the details then."

"Will you be able to run in this? I don't think Ghost will be stupid enough to swallow the bait all the way up to your fists." This concern raised questions in Isabella's mind as well.

"If I leave it open like this" — Liam now showed bits of his man cleavage — "I can pull it off in a matter of seconds."

"Ghost is pretty fast and strong. I've been on top of him and I can testify that he threw me off with ease. And what if he has a weapon?" Dan sounded pessimistic. She wasn't there when Liam took Ghost the first time they met. Unlike her, Dan had no idea that Liam was more than capable if things got physical.

"I think my military training will be more than sufficient should it come to that," Liam said in a cool voice. Dan scoffed and was about to say something when Liam cut her off.

"Delta Force training, to be precise." Liam nodded over to Dan in an even cooler tone now, if that was even possible. Dan closed her mouth, putting an end to any doubt about his abilities.

"You were in the Delta Force?"

Liam carefully took off the dress, revealing the t-shirt and shorts he wore underneath. "Sorry to shatter your *rosy* views about me, but just because someone is good at cooking and doesn't blow hot air every time he opens his mouth doesn't mean he's a loser either."

Dan looked like a child that had just been schooled by her teacher.

"What is a Delta Force?" Isabella's brows were drawn together. She had never heard of this Delta Force that had caused Dan to be so speechless for the first time since she'd known her.

"They're one of the most elite military task forces on the planet. Very few survive just to earn the rank. They are trained with a very specific set of skills—counterterrorism—so they can deal with enemies of the state."

"Oh." Isabella was impressed. "Like the Spartans?"

Dan nodded. "Exactly like the Spartans. They come back with their shield or on it—no in between."

Isabella looked at the man who literally just moments ago had stood in a dress in front of her. The same man who made pancakes with smiley faces and treated a cat like it was the king of the world. But then she also remembered the man who took out Ghost with one blow and held her in his rock-hard body of steel all night after they made love, so no, she didn't doubt him to be a Spartan at all.

"I was as lucky as I was young." Liam folded the dress and placed it on the table. "Those days are behind me now. There are more important things in life to take care of." He gave Isabella an intense look.

Somehow, she knew what he meant. To come home to someone waiting for him. To start a family. To love and be loved. All the things her heart craved as much as the flowers craved the sun. She was so busy with everything that had happened that she totally forgot what *going home* actually meant. Isabella stared at the man of her dreams, the love of her life. Then her gaze gradually lowered, staring at the floor with empty eyes. When all of this was over, she would never see Liam again.

"Well then. I'm actually confident now that this little stunt of yours will catch that damn Ghost. When do you want to set the trap?" Dan asked.

"Tomorrow," Isabella heard herself, amazed that she had just said that.

"You might be right." Dan wrinkled her nose. "The sooner the better. This Ghost isn't stupid. Who knows for how much longer he'll be following me around before he starts realizing that it's all a trap?"

Liam didn't look at her, nor did he do anything to protest. "Great, tomorrow then," he confirmed in a voice so casual it sounded as if he was setting up a time for having tea. Did he not understand what this meant? Or did he simply not care? Had he grown tired of all her time travel drama? Her heart felt crumpled, sinking into itself like a deflating balloon.

"I better go. I don't want to return home too late or the Ghost might start wondering what I am up to."

"Of course." Isabella tried to sound as normal as Liam did as they walked Dan to the door.

"Be ready around nine. That is the usual time him and I start playing cat and mouse. I will text you for confirmation."

"Ok. You know what to do. I will be waiting on the grass behind the lavatories." Liam gave Dan an affirmative look.

"Right next to the trees?"

"Yes. This gives him plenty of cover to see me in the dress and hopefully think I'm Isabella. Plus, I can keep an eye on Isabella inside the car from the parking lot right next to the field."

"I agree. He might actually be smarter than we think. It's better to have a constant view of her." Dan turned toward her for a brief moment. Isabella felt a sting in her ear. She didn't like how they were planning her every move, but it was the most logical thing to do, so there was no reason for her to argue.

As she was about to leave the house, Dan turned to Isabella and looked at her like a mother would look at her own child. Though she rarely showed it, it was obvious that Dan was worried and even sad. The time they had left together would soon come to an end. Isabella wondered, would they still remember her, or would she be forgotten through time? Would she disappear in this timeline like she never existed at all?

"I'll see you tomorrow," Isabella said, trying to hide her face. Dan nodded and closed the door behind herself. Liam and Isabella stood in the hallway, frozen in place. The quiet around them seemed very loud; it was deafening as they both stared in different directions. Liam turned toward her first, but before he could say something, Isabella started walking toward the bedroom with determined steps.

"I will get some rest now, tomorrow is a big day." Her voice sounded toneless.

Liam didn't follow her. She barely made it into the bedroom before the by now all too familiar burning sensation of tears appeared. The thought of never seeing him again was breaking her heart. But there was another thought running through her mind over and over again, slowly eating away at her soul. The thought grew louder and louder until it sounded like her own heartbeat. A thought worse than the nightmare of leaving Liam behind forever. It was the thought of him not caring that she left.

CHAPTER 15

L iam decided it would be best to show up to the river park early to go over the plan one more time. He still had to choose the best location to turn himself into a human guinea pig. Isabella had no idea how well—or not—Liam had slept last night, but she herself was up a lot, thanks to anxious thoughts and nightmares. Her worries ran around her head in circles, like vultures ready to tear her flesh apart, to break her out from this fantasy world, and back to the misery that awaited her in 1881.

There was nothing she would have wished for more than for Liam to kick the door open and comfort her in his warm, strong arms. To make her believe that there was a future, a world in time where both of them could be together. It was killing her inside, driving her mad, not knowing if Liam still felt the same way about her...or was he more eager to set her free? But as much as it would break her heart, she couldn't blame him for wanting his life back and things to return to normal. No passion in the world could possibly compete with the calm he would be able to live as soon as she was gone. No coin shops, no Mamas, no big silly dresses, and no Ghost. What a calm and normal life indeed.

Isabella almost didn't want to get out of bed. What was it all for? To return to Lord Warrington and her despicable mother? And just when she almost decided to call it off, to stay here in the twenty-first century, the memory of her brother packing his travel trunks flashed in front of her. Servants were buzzing around like frightened little flies. His mother screaming at him whether or not he had gone mad.

"Not as mad as marrying my beloved sister to that monster," he yelled back at his mother. He lovingly grabbing Isabella's hand while he spoke the last words she would ever hear from him. "I shall make things right, even if it takes my last breath. I shall make things right..." It was the last time she ever saw him.

The same morning, he left for the voyage toward the Wild West to mine for gold, leaving nothing behind but letters that arrived months late at a time. No. Isabella had to go back to him, or she would never forgive herself. With a heavy heart, she rolled herself out of bed and got dressed.

After an awkward breakfast during which both of them acted so formal one might think they were business partners, Liam headed out to Brunswick's lawyer to sign the paperwork that would give him the sole ownership of his company. By the time he finally got back home, it was already getting dark.

The last remaining time burned slowly as they waited for Dan's text. They would go over tonight's mission again and again and again, including several alternative scenarios in case something should go wrong, which in this case always led to Liam hammering the same instructions into Isabella that he probably would have tattooed onto her if he could.

DO NOT LEAVE THE CAR. KEEP THE DOORS LOCKED. NO MATTER WHAT. CALL 911. DO NOT LEAVE THE CAR. KEEP THE DOORS LOCKED. NO MATTER WHAT. CALL 911…

Liam had her repeat the words so often, she would probably dream about them tonight, and the next, for the rest of her life.

They both sat at the table in silence, each to their own thoughts, when the phone sounded. It was a text from Dan.

I think he is close. Get ready.

261

An ice-cold shiver ran down her spine, her heart picking up speed. Liam reached out, about to grab her hand, but reluctantly pulled his hand back to his side.

"Don't worry. I won't let anything happen to you."

Isabella's hands turned limp as she stared at him with rejected eyes, wanting to look away.

"You ready?" he asked almost in a whisper.

Isabella nodded with a heavy heart.

Liam pulled into a small parking lot next to the grass fields where he would be waiting for Dan, hopefully being followed by Ghost. He was wearing the dress over a gray-colored jogging outfit that allowed him to move freely. It was almost pitch black with no lights close by, except for the one mounted to the wall of a lavatory building at the end of the parking lot. Even there, the light was dim and clearly broken as it pulsed on and off at unpredictable intervals. It gave a rather eerie vibe. A perfect place to commit a crime.

Liam turned off the engine and threw his head back. Isabella tried to figure out what was on his mind. Something felt off. Was he nervous?

"It's perfectly all right to be scared," she almost whispered.

She had spoken before she even realized what she had said. Gosh, what would she give if she could just lean over and put her head onto his shoulder. To steal just one more moment before all of this began, and ended at the same time.

Liam looked out the window.

"I'm not scared. Not of Ghost." What did that mean? She was about to ask him when her phone lit up. It was Dan.

Ready now. I'm on my way. Ten minutes.

Liam reached under his seat and pulled out a knife. Its silver blade reflected the glow from her phone and onto his face. He pulled his leg up and placed the knife in some form of a black holster wrapped around his ankle. Isabella felt a tight knot form in her stomach, growing denser, twisting harder as the seconds ticked away. This wasn't a game. Things could get ugly. What if Liam got hurt?

"Remember, keep the doors locked at all times. If even the slightest thing goes wrong, call the police immediately. And do not get out." His voice was firm and as serious as it could get. Liam popped the door open, taking a step out when Isabella reached over to grab his arm.

Tell him.

Her throat went dry.

Bloody hell!

Her mouth parted.

Tell him that you love him…

Liam stared at her. Waiting. Confused.

"Be careful," she heard herself say.

Coward!

Liam nodded with a determined look on his face. He closed the door behind him and waited for her to lock the car from the inside. And just like that, he disappeared into the darkness of the field, leaving nothing else for her to watch but a silhouette in the distance.

She pressed her face against the window to get a better look, but his car had some sort of a dark film attached to it. On one hand it was great as it made it almost impossible for her to be seen from the outside, but on the other hand it made it harder for her to keep an eye on Liam. For the thousandth time, her eyes kept staring at the radio clock. It was almost nine thirty. Liam still stood in the middle of the field, and her eyes were about to wander off to her phone, when she saw Dan in front of the lavatory standing under its dim, flickering light for the whole world to see.

Cold sweat formed on her forehead. This was really happening! Just as they'd planned, Dan looked from left to right, pretending she was making sure she wasn't being followed. She stepped out of the light to wave at Liam, who did a pretty good job waving back like a lady would, barely moving his arm and shaking his hand instead.

Dan slowly made her way over the field. Isabella bit her lips, breathing heavily as she felt her veins jumping under her skin. But there was no sign of Ghost. She felt her heart shrinking in a mixture of disappointment and relief. *Where the bloody hell was he?*

This might be her one chance at catching him before the police would, making it impossible to ever get in touch with him. Her mind played with that idea for a moment. Wouldn't that mean that she couldn't go back home? That she would *have to* stay? In that case, she had tried everything in her power to find a way back to 1881 but had simply failed. A strange feeling of relief overcame her. Ghost was nowhere to be seen and Dan was only a few meters from Liam now, both safe and sound. Yes, this was it. This would mean she could stay. She tried hard but still failed. Instead of returning to a life of misery at the side of Lord Warrington and her unbearable mother, she could now stay here. With Dan...and Liam! And maybe he would start to come around as soon as all her time travel drama had stopped. Of course she still felt terrible for her brother, and always would, but it was not like she didn't try—quite the opposite!

A smile crossed her lips, followed by butterflies in her stomach. She felt light on her feet, wanting to burst out of the car and run as fast as she could toward them. She grabbed her phone, ready to call Dan and tell her this was it, this was finally it, she could stay and that everything would be okay, when she caught something moving in the corner of her eye. Her heart jumped against her chest, pounding loudly on her ribcage. She jerked around, trying to get a better view in the darkness, pressing her face against the window as the lights in the distance flickered on and off. On and off. On and— there! There he was! Ghost! The shadow of the night that had an entire neighborhood on the edge.

There was no mistaking. This was his silhouette, pressed against the dark corner of the building, blending in with the night, slowly sneaking his way up onto the field. Isabella leaned closer, staring with blinking eyes. Something felt off. Had they even noticed him? But then Liam would surely be aware of him, considering his elite training. Isabella's whole body was cold, feeling the sharp pulses of her heavy beating heart. Ghost was several feet onto the field inching his way toward them. It was only a matter of time before he got close enough for Liam to tackle him down. But all of a sudden, out of nowhere, Ghost stopped. Before Isabella could even blink, he turned around and ran off, disappearing into the dark again like the shadow he was. Dan and Liam still stood on the field as if they hadn't even noticed he was there.

Isabella unlocked her phone to ring Dan, but Dan didn't pick up. She just stood there waiting like a desperate fisherman trying to bring home the catch that was never there in the first place.

"Please, why aren't you answering," she mumbled hectically. Dan still didn't bother to pick up. Was her phone broken? She had to tell them. Let them know he was just here. What if he's still close by?

She placed her hand on the door handle, but froze as Liam's words invaded her mind as if it was a spell that had just taken a hold of her. NO MATTER WHAT, DO NOT GET OUT.

"Bloody hell," she cussed and opened the door, placing her foot on soiled ground. She was about to get out with a hand still on the handle opening the door wider, when something dragged her back inside, pulling her entire weight like it was nothing. The door slammed shut in front of her, drowning every possible noise that managed to escape from her mouth, until that too was shut tight. She felt a heavy hand pressed onto her mouth from behind her, holding it tightly shut.

"I won't hurt you," she heard a whisper as if those words were never spoken. Or were they?

The car shuddered. The headlights turned on. It took a second, still facing the passenger's window, until Isabella noticed that Ghost was sitting behind her on the driver's seat. Using his free arm that was not holding her in place, he started the car and put it into drive, hastily hitting the gas pedal. He was dressed all in black, even wearing a black mask. The car revved in an angry, loud growl and shot a few feet forward, ready to drive off. But all of a sudden, the car stopped again, growling and slowly rolling forward to a complete halt. Isabella finally realized that Ghost had released her from what felt like a deathly grip and jerked around to find the driver's seat empty and the car door wide open. She scrambled to open the door to her side and quickly jumped out to see Liam, without the dress, holding a tall dark figure to the ground, illuminated by the blaring bright headlights that flashed before them. Ghost bellowed in pain, tried to roll over to get back up, but Liam had him by the neck with the other arm held on his back, pushing him down with his full weight on top of him.

"Are you okay?" Liam shouted over to Isabella without taking his eyes off his catch. In the distance, Dan was slowly making her way up from the field. Liam must have outrun her like a cheetah would a sloth.

"Yes, I'm fine." She managed to speak. She wasn't so sure of that moments ago. Her heart was still racing, but at least she was alive.

"Who are you?" Liam yelled at Ghost in a deep soldier type of voice that sounded threatening and scary at the same time.

Ghost didn't answer, which resulted in Liam tightening his grip around his neck. Ghost tried every move possible to wiggle his way out of Liam's iron hold, but it didn't budge at all. Isabella couldn't help but be in awe of how strong Liam was. His veins were popping out from his wrist running through his entire steel-like arm. *He truly is a Spartan.* To come to her rescue so quickly and outrun a car, then to tackle this man like a tiger would overwhelm a rabbit, it was nothing short of jaw dropping.

"I won't ask you this nicely again."

Liam tightened his grip even further, causing Ghost to scream out in pain and agony. Isabella gasped. Never had she seen Liam this angry before.

"Why are you trying to hurt me?" Isabella yelled.

"I—," Ghost suddenly coughed much to everybody's surprise. "I'm not trying—"

Wait! Was that a British accent? How did they miss that the first time?

Ghost continued, which wasn't easy with Liam's hand wrapped around his throat. "Not trying to hurt you—" *Cough.* "Lady Astley..."

LADY ASTLEY? Her hand shot up to her mouth, utterly flabbergasted. "What did you just say?" she shouted, stepping closer.

"Isabella...Astley. Sister... Of the former Duke of Aberdeen."

This couldn't be! What was going on? Liam loosened his grip, obviously confused as well, but not confused enough to just let go of him. Ghost gasped for air, coughing wildly, but focused his attention onto talking again.

"I'm not here to hurt you," he said gasping in short, quick breaths.

"Who are you?!" Dan said in a harsh raspy voice like she was ready to cast a curse on him, but Ghost kept quiet.

"Well, let's start with this."

Liam tore off his black mask, revealing a young blond man who looked no older than twenty. Some would even consider him rather handsome. Isabella raised her eyebrows, blinking away a peculiar thought. She had the strange feeling that she knew this man. Well he obviously knew who she was. But how? Did her mother send him?

"It's okay, Liam." She gently placed a hand onto his steel-hard arm that held Ghost in place.

"You sure?" Liam said with a pinched expression.

She nodded. Liam grimaced. "Don't even think about doing something stupid." Liam slowly softened his grip. Ghost stumbled forward, coughing and rubbing his throat that had now turned red where Liam had squeezed the life out of him.

"No shit," he sneered back with a gaze that flicked upward. His accent was without a doubt British.

"What do you want from our Isabella?" Dan crossed her arms, impatiently pacing in place. Ghost looked up at her, seemingly unperturbed, and didn't say a word. Liam lurched forward and swung his right-hand fist into his left palm, making an audible threatening sound.

"I must have given you the impression that you don't have to answer us... Let me fix that."

Ghost stumbled backward, almost falling into Isabella. "Wait," she interrupted, holding her hand up. He gave her a thankful gaze. "Nobody will hurt you; I promise. But you will have to answer our questions."

"Let's start with why you've been following her." Dan snickered, growing more impatient by the second.

Ghost stared at them for a moment, debating about the pros and cons of talking. "I can't. Not while the others are here," he finally said.

"Why not?" Isabella asked.

Ghost kept quiet again. Liam, on the other hand, was done playing games. He walked up to Ghost who jerked both his fists up to his face.

"Don't be ridiculous," Liam rolled his eyes. He grabbed Ghost by one of his wrists and swung him around while twisting his arm onto his back, placing him into a police hold. Ghost didn't dare to move a muscle as it would just cause pain. Liam reached into Ghost's black jean pocket and pulled out a wallet.

"Not very wise bringing that," he said sarcastically.

He flipped it open with his free hand to look at it while Isabella and Dan watched in anticipation. His eyes widened like an owl while his posture stiffened. A sudden rush of blood ran through his face in awe. He was so surprised that he let go of Ghost without even realizing it.

"What is it?" Isabella and Dan spoke in chorus, taking a step closer.

Liam was at a loss for words along with an unfocused gaze that blinked faster and faster, like he was trying to wake himself up from slumber. Isabella managed to break him out from his daze.

He wasn't even aware that he had handed the wallet to Isabella, whose mouth now also slackened to the floor, pressing her hand against her chest, fingers grasping on to the fabric of her clothes. She slowly looked up toward the man who stood in front of them, then quickly shifted her gaze back to the wallet she held in her slightly trembling hands.

"H-henry?" Isabella struggled to find her voice as she swallowed the lump that formed in her throat. "Your name is Henry? Henry...Astley?" Isabella gasped as she just heard herself say her own name.

"The Duke of Aberdeen, at least according to Google." Liam stared at his phone, shaking his head in confusion.

Henry threw his head back in despair. "This is going so terribly wrong!" He spoke into the clear night sky, sounding desperate.

"Could somebody here help me out on this one? I hate being the stupid one in the group," Dan interrupted, wrinkling her forehead.

"He is my, um, my... We are related, apparently." Isabella stuttered as her legs almost gave in.

"You're related?" Dan stepped closer, analyzing him from head to toe with her big eyes under half broken glasses. "Yes. I can see that now." She turned toward Isabella with her brows perked up. "But how?"

"A rather distant relation, I'm afraid," Henry finally joined in.

"He even sounds like you. A modern version of you," Dan said, nodding confirmation of her own words.

Isabella was still in shock when Henry walked up to her to pull his wallet out of her hands. "If you don't mind," he said, putting it back into his pocket. It was dead silent for the moment. The cold breeze of the night blew in their faces as they stood in front of the car's headlights, a fitting metaphor for the darkness that had shrouded them all for weeks, now gathered to find the light and the truth in all of this.

Everyone was deep in their own thoughts, until Dan broke the silence. "So, you are a noblewoman?"

Isabella shook her head. "I used to be, but I am of no importance any longer."

"You must be joking!" Henry shouted in an odd voice while his fist shot into the air like he was an actor in some sort of drama. "Tell me you are joking!"

"About what?" She wrinkled her forehead, completely lost inside her thoughts. Henry studied her with his chin held high, trying to see if she really meant what she'd just said. Then he put his hands to his hips like a teacher scolding a pupil. "So, you have no idea about the family's oath. Absolutely none whatsoever?"

"The what?" Isabella stared at him with raised eyebrows and a slackened jaw.

"I guess it makes sense considering you've only been here for a month. Which, by the way, *is* getting rather very close."

Liam and Isabella exchanged looks but weren't too surprised that he knew about her time travel. At this point it seemed more and more likely that Henry might even know more about all of this than any of them.

"Close to what?" Liam asked.

Henry took in a deep breath, held it, and forced the air back out. "Bloody hell. Things are going totally wrong here anyway." He calmly walked over to Isabella and stopped right in front of her, catching her gaze. "Your brother. I was sent by your brother."

Isabella lifted her hand to her mouth in a mixture of relief and confusion. "George? Is he here?"

Henry shook his head and stared into the darkness. "No, not like that. After you disappeared in 1881, George dropped everything overnight and started looking for you. He was out of himself, obsessed with finding you. People thought his sorrow turned him mad. Maybe it really did for a while."

She felt a sharp pain spread across her chest like someone had just stabbed her with a knife. Isabella pressed a hand to her breast as if to stop the blood from seeping through. She was right about her poor brother. His suffering. His pain. He would have never rested, turning the world inside out to find her.

"How terrible!" She grabbed Henry by the shoulders. "I have to return! Please help me!"

Henry looked at her empathetically and pulled out an envelope with nothing written on it. "I think you should read this first." He handed it to her. It looked clearly old with its yellowish, stained color and almost rough texture. "It actually looked pretty decent for its age until I had to chase you down for the past four weeks. Hiding in bushes, wrestling…"

He threw Dan and Liam quick sharp look, "It made it age more in four weeks than it did in the hundred and forty years it's been in the family's possession."

Isabella felt her heart leaping from her chest as she frantically tore the envelope open and leaned it toward the headlight.

"My Dearest Sister...," she read out loud.

I can only hope that this letter finds you well. You cannot imagine the joy I felt when I was informed that you are still alive. I also hope you will forgive me that I have blamed our mother for your disappearance at first, which as you might already assume, she did not take too fondly.

I have spent many years looking for you. I have traveled the world, following one lead after the next... I was blaming myself, going mad! "Mad George" is what society called me behind closed doors over a cup of tea and a piece of lemon cake. But please do not be alarmed, as fate has its own way of jesting, and in this case, the rumours about Mad George ultimately brought me peace—in the form of Lady Emma Washington, an American woman claiming to be from the future and insisting I use her maiden name to write to you. She stated that she'd heard about Mad George's tragedy at a dinner party and knew instantly that the two of you must be connected in some way. After more research, she came to know that the two of you somehow traded places. At first, I thought her just as mad as myself, but after she presented me with the most marvellous device, named cellular phone, I believed her every word. She also brought a newspaper boy with her that bore witness to your disappearance in the middle of the road like magic.

I have left careful instructions for my descendants to guard this letter, tying my estate and fortune to a trust fund. Its inheritance is based on the condition that this letter will be passed down and stay in the family until it reaches you safely, or the entire estate shall be gifted to the veteran's fund. And there is much to give away. Fate has favoured me again... Although I never found gold, I did find love, Isabella. She is wonderful; you two would get along splendidly. She is American and the heiress of an oil empire. Mother was very pleased, as you might already have guessed. Not so much about the part of the small cottage we exiled her to, as well as a more than adequate allowance, but mother will always be mother, and I had no intention of letting her spend us into ruin ever again.

My dear sister, although I am deeply relieved, I am also deeply worried at the same time. What if you are struggling in this strange new world? From Lady Washington's description, it sounds rather overwhelming. What if you want to come home, scared and all alone?

Lady Washington agreed with me that you should at least have the chance to return to your home in 1881, if you so choose. Therefore, she offered to try to trade places again. Her plan is to replay the events of that fateful night on this upcoming Thursday, which should be exactly a month from when you arrived in Philadelphia. At exactly 23:35 your time, she will be bending over for a Victorian shilling, right where the newspaper boy claimed you have disappeared. She did refuse to tell me if she wanted to return home to the twenty-first century or not, stating that she did not want to influence your decision to remain or return. She is a kind and admirable lady, Isabella. I am shocked as to how much she reminds me of you.

With this being said, my dear sister, I will wait for you on Thursday, December 17th, at the 23:35 hour.

With all my love,

Your Brother George

For how long Isabella stood there staring at the letter, no one could tell, since everyone was as stunned as she was. Isabella finally managed to tear herself away from it, looking at Henry who was patiently waiting for her to take it all in.

"He never gave up," she almost whispered.

Henry wrinkled his forehead. "Gave up? Did you not read the letter? The whole estate and Aberdeen fortune is tied to you, to this day. Everyone after George was entrusted with this family secret. It was like an oath. Honestly…," he said scratching his head, "I couldn't even begin to tell you what would have happened to the estate if I hadn't managed to finally find you."

"Well, maybe you shouldn't have stalked her like a creep and just talked to her, like a real man would," Dan sneered.

"You mean missing out on weeks on the streets, chased by cops and drug dealers, beaten up by army boy here while constantly lingering around 5th Street like a pervert in the cold?" Henry sneered back, sighed, then focused his gaze back to Isabella. "It's not like I didn't try. The night Isabella arrived, I was ready. But then Rambo here took me out. All of this had to happen quietly, without anybody involved. Isabella was supposed to stay with me, hidden, until she returned back home. Number one rule of time travel, leave no imprints behind. Unless you want to alter world events into unpredictable and catastrophic proportions."

Henry looked up into the clear dark sky like he was trying to find something from the great void up above as he cleared his throat. "But that's all out the window now. Everything just went horribly wrong. I'm revealed and Isabella now walks and talks like a modern lady."

Liam moved closer to Isabella, leaning closer toward her. "What if it doesn't work? How would the duke know she received the letter but couldn't travel back for whatever reasons?" he asked Henry.

Isabella lifted her head curiously, immediately understood what Liam implied but was more anxious of Henry's answer, if there was any.

"He had a piece of paper with the answer to a question only the two of you would know. He locked it away in a bank security deposit box. If this letter reaches you but the whole-time travel thing doesn't work, then I can still prove that I did my duty by providing the answer to this question correctly. The bank will then release the estate from all conditions."

Dan seemed amused by this. "And if you fail to have the answer, then all your bling will be gone?"

It was very obvious on Henry's face that he didn't like where the conversation was heading. He stared at the ground and nodded, before staring Dan in the eye. "Every last cent of it. My bloody great-great-grandfather made sure we wouldn't neglect trying to find his long-lost sister. That itself is for sure."

As everything slowly settled in, Isabella was overcome by a sudden feeling of great joy. The sparkle in her eyes returned, and her face lit up like a light bulb. Her brother was well, he had fallen in love, had children! He didn't spend the last of his days looking for her in utter misery like she feared he would. She felt bubbles fill her stomach with an uncontrollable upturned face. She was so elated that she threw her arms around Henry, who flinched a few steps back with a curled shoulder, thinking he was being held into another choke hold.

"All of this is so wonderful!" Isabella was laughing and crying at the same time. "I can't thank you enough!" She looked over to Liam, wanting to tell him how happy she was for her brother. That the feeling of guilt that she'd carried for such a long time had evaporated in a single instant. That maybe now that she knew her brother was okay, finally she could st—

"I agree. It's great that you can finally go back home tomorrow, and everything goes back to normal," Liam said in a cold voice.

Isabella slowly let go of Henry. Her smile vanished into a blank empty stare as she unknowingly took a few steps back. What did he just say? Did Liam really want her to go back? Granted, it would give him his old, *normal* life back. And now that he had his company to return to, it only made sense that he would want to dive back into the work that he loved so much, surrounded by people that he cared for.

She had been and still was new to this world. Even without the whole time travel drama, Isabella was still a high maintenance person to have around. Just until yesterday she didn't even know that Burger King wasn't owned by actual royalty. She turned away to hide her face, not wanting her tears to be seen, as they were no longer tears of joy.

"Back to normal, that would be lovely," she responded, trying to keep her voice from trembling.

"Splendid," Henry echoed her pretend happiness in innocent ignorance. "I'm pleased to hear that everybody believes in her return."

"I don't," Dan threw in her two cents. "Why can't she choose to stay?"

"Well first of all, she obviously doesn't want to," Henry countered firmly but in a kind tone.

Dan frowned at him, unconvinced in the least.

"Then there is also the case with the other girl, Emma. She wouldn't tell us about her, so how do we know that she is not trying desperately to go back home?" he added.

Dan opened her mouth ready to defy Henry, but Isabella interrupted her.

"He is right, Dan," she said in a soft, yielding voice. And with Liam who seemed to agree with her leaving, and the several good points that Henry had made, it seemed to be the only choice. What if Emma was as desperate as her when she first arrived in this strange world, eagerly waiting at the agreed location tomorrow, wishing her heart away to return home? She didn't belong in this world. None of this was supposed to happen. She was never supposed to meet Dan, or Jerry or…Liam. After all, she was never supposed to be here.

"Tomorrow I shall return home," Isabella said under pursed lips, looking up from her downturned gaze to take a quick short glance at where Liam stood.

"Well in that case, let's go back home and get your things packed and what not." Liam walked off toward the car.

"Actually…" Henry interrupted, "Isabella should come with me. There is much to discuss regarding tomorrow. And some other important things we need to go over. In private, of course. None of this was supposed to happen this way in the first place. She was supposed to leave no footprints behind in this world."

Liam threw a quick glance at Isabella, hiding away his clenched jaw that throbbed under his cheek. "Yes, that makes sense."

They both looked away, not wanting to see the face of the other. Not wanting to make guesses on how the other one felt.

"Just call me later and keep me posted. I'll meet you at the location tomorrow and bring your things if you want me to."

Dan looked back and forth between the two of them, throwing a sharp gaze at the brief moment that unfolded in front of her. She could tell how incredibly awkward they were.

"Yes, of course," Isabella said.

Liam finally directed his gaze back at her, almost as if something had nailed him to the floor and he was unable to leave without looking at her one more time. For that brief moment, it was as if time had stood still for him, forever imprinted into his mind and his heart. He shook his head and turned around to get back in the car. And just like that, he drove off.

Dan grabbed Isabella's hand and squeezed it gently, leaning over to whisper, "Tomorrow we'll talk to him. It's not what it seems like. I'm sure." She was obviously trying her best to comfort her.

Isabella's sadness and desperation must have been written all over her face. How did Liam not notice that?

Her gaze followed him. Her legs beneath her slowly carried her toward the direction the car had taken off, until they stopped, refusing to take another step until he was out of sight. What if he wouldn't even show up tomorrow? Would he just abandon her? What if this was the last time she would ever get to see him?

There was no doubt in her mind that her broken heart would never mend.

CHAPTER 16

He watched her from the rear-view mirror, as if she was trapped in time. Even though he could barely see her face, he remembered it as if he was standing there right in front of her. He remembered every curve of her face, every curl of her hair, every stare from her deep blue eyes, and every smile from her lips. Every memory that tormented his heart made him gasp for air. His eyes wept as every breath from his chest was being sucked out from his lungs. It became painful to see her hazy silhouette cast a shadow in the dark, but he kept his eyes on Isabella nonetheless, until she was gone.

Standing there listening to her words, he couldn't take it any longer. The pain of her leaving him just like that, smiling over the fact she'd be going back home, hurt. It hurt like nothing had ever hurt before. Not that he didn't understand where she was coming from. Of course she wanted to go back home, to see her brother, to live in her own world. But that she was so overjoyed with happiness about it shattered his heart into millions of pieces. For days he'd carried this heavy curtain of sadness on his shoulders, and tonight was just more than he could take.

When he first heard Isabella read that letter, for a brief moment, he felt hope form in the deepest corner of his heart. Isabella had always said that she would have to go back to save her brother from a life of misery. But now that they knew he was okay, Liam thought she might change her mind and stay. But that hope was blown up like a sand castle by a tsunami. She laughed, her face lit up, she looked as happy as when they'd made love to each other. But this time he wasn't the cause of her happiness. Maybe getting far away from him and this world were the reasons for her cheerful mood. How could he have been so wrong about her feelings? He really thought she cared for him. For days he had been torturing himself by supporting her decisions. The truth was, for days he'd wanted to pull her into his arms, passionately kiss her, and tell her he would not let her go. But why make it harder on her? So he'd kept telling himself whenever the urge to kiss her arose—which was every darn minute he was with her. But that was all over now as he watched her rejoice over returning to 1881.

Liam pulled over to the side of the road. He could no longer drive. His hands fell limp, falling to his side. He leaned into the car seat with his head pulled back and with a blank stare directed at the car ceiling as if he could see the sky. He tried to hold back until he couldn't, and all he could do was scream. Liam yelled, hitting the steering wheel with his fist until his hands gave up on him. He checked his phone, hoping she'd called or left a message. Checking over and over, for nothing.

"You fool…," he whispered to himself. Maybe he should just let her go now. Not even bother to show up or to say goodbye tomorrow. She might not even care anyway. There was no reason for him to stand there like an idiot, waving her farewell, and then cry out in the street for the whole world to see as the woman he loved disappeared forever. Liam checked his phone for one last time. Nothing. He threw his phone toward the passenger seat.

"Fuck!"

It was eleven thirty. Isabella, Dan, and Henry got to 5th Street early to make sure they had enough time to go over every little detail again. It was a cold, clear night. For the first time, for what seemed like forever, Isabella was wearing her Victorian dress again. Henry and Isabella had picked it up from Liam's apartment in the morning. Much to her surprise and shock, Liam wasn't there and left his key under his doormat, stating he was occupied with an urgent meeting at the office. But to Isabella it seemed more as if he was avoiding her, and the pain that it left was unbearable, deeply etched into her heart. *How did it get to this?*

Dan scanned her from head to toe, nodding in approval. She looked like a true Victorian lady again. Dan had tried to return the necklace and earrings that she had safeguarded for her, but Isabella insisted they were a gift, so she gratefully put them back in her pocket, holding on to them as if they would give her the strength she needed to see her beloved child go.

Isabella let out an exhausted sigh. The last weeks were nothing short of tiring. Constantly chasing leads, her feelings for Liam, time travel... It had all left a mark on her. It didn't help either that she was up all night. She and Henry had spent all night talking. Not in a romantic way, but as family. Isabella learned that Henry had lost both of his parents very young and that a close family friend had raised him, doing everything he could to turn him into a worthy duke, including his responsibility to fulfil his family's oath and find Isabella. As weird as it was, they both agreed there was a connection between the two of them. The kind of connection between people of the same blood. They exchanged stories about their family, the estate, Britain, and her time travel to America. Henry's cheerful nature and colorful tales managed to distract her from her depressed mood—for a few seconds here and there, that is.

Isabella looked down to check her phone for the millionth time.

"Nothing?" Dan leaned over to her, carefully fixing the ruffles in her dress, and gently pulling back the few strands of hair on her forehead.

"No." Her voice trembled. She tried to sound normal, but that was simply impossible. She couldn't hide her sorrow, even if her life depended on it. With an excruciating smile, she handed her phone back to Dan.

"I won't need it any longer."

Dan gently pushed it back to Isabella. "There is still a bit of time. He might still call…"

Isabella shook her head with tears rolling down her face. The sorrow was slowly eating away at her. She could only pray that this agonizing pain would subside with time, as she otherwise had no idea how she could ever begin to manage it.

"He won't. And I can't blame him," she almost whispered, looking down onto the floor.

Henry stepped right next to Isabella, taking away the phone. Her heart sank as the only thing left that she held from this time disappeared from her grasp.

"I don't want to be the bad guy, but there is no more time. We have to get in position."

Isabella nodded as her gaze turned toward the street, scanning for something that wasn't there. "Yes, of course." She forced her gaze toward Henry like ripping away a part of the past. "Thank you for everything you and your ancestors have done for me. I want to apologize for my brother's more than inconvenient inheritance arrangements."

Henry sympathetically put his hand on her shoulder. "Please don't. After all, he was just watching out for family. Our family." He gave her a warm smile. "And it made us sort of interesting. I mean, how many other dukes can claim time travelers in their family?"

Isabella smiled back at him. It was quite incredible. All these generations later and her brother's kind heart was still running in the family. Dan checked the time. "Geez...we gotta hurry! It's 11:35."

Without wasting another second, Isabella threw herself around Dan's neck, holding her close for one final moment. This woman had shared what little she had with her, cared for her, and unconditionally loved her. Tears flowed down both of their cheeks.

"Dan, I will never forget you. Thank you for everything you have done for me."

Dan squeezed her tightly for the last time before releasing her. "Go now, and show those 1881 abusive male pricks that they can't mess around with a street-smart girl from Philly." Dan shook her fist.

"I promise." She smiled at her warmly.

With the heaviest heart a woman could possibly carry, Isabella squeezed Dan for a final time before letting go. She walked into the middle of the road, right where she had first woken up in the arms of the man she would never see again. A man she loved dearly. A man who meant the world to her beyond time and space.

Dan placed the Victorian shilling in front of her, moving several steps back as if there would be some sort of explosion about to happen. Isabella threw her head back and looked up to the sky. She could see the stars shining brightly above her. She came into this world as a spoiled entitled girl and would leave as a strong, independent woman. Then she closed her eyes.

If I could just see him one more time…

"Now!" Henry's voice echoed in the background.

Just once…

"You have to wish to return! It's eleven thirty-five." Dan joined Henry's cries.

Isabella opened her eyes. Her gaze cascaded beneath her where the coin glinted next to her feet. She bent over to grab it, trying to focus her mind on returning home. She braced herself as her hand reached over, and then she noticed something just at the corner of her eye. Was her mind playing tricks on her? Right in the middle of the road, just a few feet away from her, there he was! Her touch just inches away from the coin. Liam! But before she could stop, before she could cry out to him, before she could take it all back, she could already feel the cold silver in her hand.

"I love you!" she heard him shout.

"I LOVE YOU!"

A strange energy took over her body like a flood swallowing the shores. The same power she felt when she first time traveled. She tried to keep her eyes open, to get a glimpse of Liam just one more time, but something forcefully pressed her eyes shut. A loud blowing sound filled her ears like a violent storm of gust and thunder engulfing her. For a moment she wished the carriage had hit her again. At least she would have time traveled unconscious; and in all of this, as scared as she had ever been before, all she could think about was Liam. His face, his smile, his tender touch. She wanted to be with him and him alone—forever.

Then all of a sudden, out of nowhere, everything came to a complete stop. She was surrounded by utter silence. For a moment she kept her eyes shut, not wanting to open them, to look and see herself back in 1881. Tears were running down her cheeks; the desperation of being back in 1881 tore her insides apart. She wanted to scream as loud as she had ever screamed before. But just when she opened her mouth to do so, she felt a gentle, warm touch on her hand, followed by the same beautiful voice that brought her into this world for the first time.

"It's okay..."

Isabella tore her eyes wide open and burst into tears. Liam was in front of her, smiling. She jerked around to find Henry and Dan right where she last saw them... At the side of 5th Street in twenty-first century Philadelphia. Her desperation and pain instantly dissolved into the air and left her with nothing but relief and pure joy.

"You came," she whispered, facing Liam again.

He gently lifted her chin, looking deep into her eyes. The all-too-familiar butterflies started to form in her stomach, tingling all the way into her fingertips. She couldn't believe it. She was still here! And it was truly him as he pulled her closer!

"I had to. The thought of never seeing you again was as good as a death sentence."

She threw herself into his arms, crying tears of joy into his shoulder. Henry and Dan now came running over.

"What happened?" Henry shouted frantically and scratching his head.

"Maybe this Emma lady didn't want to come back here." Dan shrugged her shoulders.

"Or maybe she didn't know that she had to wish for it," Henry said out loud, trying to figure out what was going on. "But why wouldn't she know —"

"It's not her," Isabella said, turning toward them. She looked down, avoiding their gazes.

"What do you mean?" Liam asked.

Isabella opened her hand to look at the coin. It was still there. "I mean it's not her fault it didn't work." She closed her fist around it again, and this time met their gazes. "It is my fault."

"But how?" Henry asked, shaking his head.

"I'm so sorry, Henry." Isabella faced him with an apology written all over her face.

"I tried. I really did. But my heart..." She looked over to Liam, meeting his beautiful eyes with hers. "My heart didn't want to leave."

Liam drew his brows in surprise. "You didn't? But I thought you wanted to leave? Return back home?"

Isabella shook her head. "Me? No. I never wanted to leave. I—I—" She tore him away. "I'm so sorry, Liam. I know you might not want me here, but I promise, I won't be in your way or bother you or—"

Before Isabella could finish her sentence, Liam swept her off her feet, then spun her around before pulling her into his embrace. His whole face lit up with joy.

298

"In my way? I won't ever let you go again!" He smiled bright and wide from ear to ear. He leaned closer and right then and there, in front of everyone, he sank his lips onto hers, kissing her passionately. A wave of tingling excitement and happiness rushed through her body, taking over every emotion she had ever felt, past and present. She gently tore away from his sweet lips, just long enough to tell him the very words that burned inside her, demanding to be spoken, right here, right now.

"Liam, I love you."

For a moment he just looked at her in awe. Then he gently ran his fingers down her flushed cheek, inching closer, breath to breath, and softly brushed his lips against hers again. "I love you too, Isabella. More than you'll ever know."

They might have just stood there and kissed all night if it hadn't been for Dan clearing her throat.

"I don't want to be the party pooper here, but we should leave before Jerry catches us. It's about the time he does his rounds around these parts. I definitely don't want to be interrogated when he finds all of us on this damn street."

"Very true," Liam said and took Isabella's hand. He wanted to start walking but she didn't move. "What is it?"

Isabella turned toward Henry. "Failure," she said to him out of nowhere.

Henry wrinkled his forehead in confusion. "Me?" He pointed at himself.

She shook her head in loud laughter. "No. The answer to the question that will release your estate. I didn't travel back so…"

Henry finally caught up. "Oh, yes. The answer to the question of what your mother used to call your father."

"Yes, the answer to that is *failure*. That should finally set you free."

Henry didn't seem to know how to respond to that, folding his hands behind his head, trying to find the right words. "My great-great-grandmother sounds absolutely…lovely."

Isabella grinned. "Oh, she was a true blessing."

It was quite incredible; despite everything that had happened, oddly enough, she almost felt grateful for her mother. She no longer hated her. Those feelings had dissolved. Now that she had finally broken free from the golden cage that had trapped her heart for so long, why hate her? Without everything that had happened between her and mother, she would have never traded places with this Emma, and would have never met Liam, Dan, and even Henry.

She could only hope that Emma was as happy in 1881 as she was here in the twenty-first century. But that was surely something they could find out by digging into the past using Google.

Isabella looked over to the very spot where she'd first woken up in Liam's arms—scared, confused, and all alone. Four weeks later, she was deeply loved, had amazing friends, and was able to let go of the rage toward her mother that had been eating her from the inside for years. She looked back one more time onto the very pavement that had changed her life and ultimately brought her happiness—and love.

"Straight roads don't make good drivers," Liam said as if he was reading her mind. He lifted her hand to his lips and gently kissed her one more time before they all walked away.

"Did you read that in one of your cooking books for man-cakes?" Dan asked with a sarcastic grin.

Henry drew his brows together, staring at them with a dazed look on his face. "What the bloody hell are man-cakes?"

They all laughed, except for Henry, of course.

"They are the way to a woman's heart, my friend. Isabella and Dan are the living proof," Liam said with a grin on his face.

Dan spat out a growl, causing the whole group to laugh again.

It was right there and then that Isabella knew she hadn't swapped places with Emma into a new, unknown world. It wasn't like that at all. It was more like she had finally returned to the place she belonged to all along. She had returned home.

EPILOGUE

Christmas Eve. Four years later...

"Mama!" little George shouted gleefully from the living room.

"I'm coming, sweetheart!" Isabella placed the movie script onto her desk. She had promised Liam she wouldn't be working on it today, but she just had the most wonderful idea that she had to make a note of before it slipped from her mind again.

It was about last year when Liam's manager introduced her to his wife, a movie producer. Several movies later, Isabella's name was the first to cross any producer's mind if they were working on a period movie and needed to be historically accurate. She loved working. It was another perk of the twenty-first century, considering that where she came from it was highly frowned upon for women of society to be employed.

Isabella left her home office and turned into the hallway when Liam pulled her aside and wrapped his arms around her. He was wearing his manly apron with a kitchen towel over his shoulder.

"I'm jealous of these movie scripts. They're getting so much of your attention." He smiled before he lowered his lips to hers, kissing her softly.

"Sounds like somebody would rather live in 1881 where men can do with their women whatever they want." She grinned seductively.

Liam kissed her again. "That sounds amazing! But then, I would probably have to eat your cooking."

She pulled away with loud laughter, playfully hitting his shoulders.

"Maaaamaaaaa!!!!" George's voice wailed from across the hallway again.

"Impatient. Just like his father." She rolled her eyes.

"He knows what he wants, you mean," Liam joked, giving her a love slap onto her butt cheeks with the kitchen towel before she could make it out of reach.

The living room was decorated most beautifully. A huge Christmas tree covered in shiny, colorful ornaments stood proudly in the corner next to the fireplace that had stockings hanging above a flickering wood fire. After Liam had turned his business around and Isabella was paid out a very large inheritance from the current Duke of Aberdeen, just as it was instructed in George's will to release the estate for good, their new Victorian four-bedroom villa in the outskirts of Philly was way below what they could afford.

"Mama!" Little George shrieked as he came running toward her.

"Look what auntie Dan got me!" He held a little toy car into the air for his mother to see.

Isabella smiled as she grabbed little George and carried him back over to where Dan was sitting on a couch. Mama was sitting next to her. Eva and Henry, on the other hand, were in the other corner of the room, deeply engaged in a heated conversation about time travel and the science behind it. Isabella leaned forward to kiss George on his cheek before gently placing him down.

"Wow, look at that. Is that auntie Dan's third Christmas gift *before* the actual gift exchange?" she said in a sweet voice, looking right above George's head and straight at Dan.

"It's just another little pre-Christmas gift." Dan crossed her arms to fight off any possible accusations of spoiling him. Dan and George had become inseparable, so much so that Liam and Isabella even had a room for her right next to George's, which was for her to come and go as she pleased.

"I don't mind, Mama." George grinned at her, skipping back onto Dan's lap.

"He doesn't mind, you hear?" Dan pulled him closer, rocking slowly back and forth with him. Isabella's heart skipped with joy seeing all these people she loved so happy.

"Isabella," Henry said, walking up to her. "I have a little pre-gift for you too." He handed her an envelope.

Her eyes widened as her mouth flopped open. "Impossible!"

She tore the envelope open to reveal a British passport.

"Never thought I would hear the word impossible from a person who literally time traveled from 1881," he jested, watching her excitement with satisfaction.

"So, they really just gave this to you?" She flipped through the pages like a little kid through a new coloring book.

"Not *just*... It took the best lawyer of London and an invitation to the Queen's annual hunting party mailed directly to the head of immigration. And voila."

She squeezed Henry as a big thank you. "You are the best!"

"Would you all stop exchanging gifts? Otherwise I will have to get mine too now and the goose won't be ready for another twenty minutes," Liam said, joining them from the kitchen, wiping his hands with a kitchen towel.

All of a sudden, Mama, who accepted every one of their invitations and was usually just watching people quietly from a corner, sat up and closed her eyes, slowly lifting both hands in the air, and spoke with her deep growling voice which they hadn't heard for quite a while now. "I see the goose in flames."

Henry rolled his eyes and opened his mouth to make a joke, when suddenly, the smoke detector went off, followed by smoke creeping into the living room. Liam turned around on the spot, storming away in an attempt to save his goose. He coughed desperately from the kitchen.

"God darn it, Mama! Next time please tell me this in advance!"

Little George crossed his arms in defense over Mama. "She just did, Daddy." His cute little voice giggled through the living room into the kitchen, followed by the loud laughter of the people who could not be more different but had come together as one—a family.

WHAT HAPPENED TO GEORGE ASTLEY?

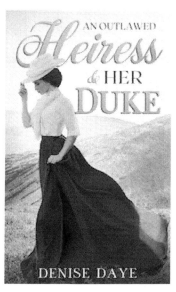

Join the Duke of Aberdeen on his incredible adventure in the historical Wild West!

The book is available on Amazon:

(FREE with Kindle Unlimited)

THANK YOU!

First of all, thank you for purchasing A Modern Lady Lost in Time. I know you could have picked any number of books to read, but you picked this book, and for that I am extremely grateful. As a small-time author and full-time mom, my readers mean the world to me!

If you enjoyed this book, it would be really nice if you could leave a review for it on Amazon.

You can review the book here:

https://www.amazon.com/dp/B084MNW7DB

Your feedback and support will help me to continue writing romance novels.

Also, don't forget to sign up for our newsletter to stay up to date on new releases and get FREE novels. You can find the newsletter and more info about our books here:

www.timelesspapers.com

Thank you!

ABOUT THE AUTHOR

Denise graduated with a Master's in Social Work from an Ivy League school and has spent many years of her life supporting families and individuals in need of assistance. She has always had a passion for writing, but it wasn't until her own baby boy was born that Denise turned her passion into her profession. Whenever Denise is not typing away on one of her books, you can find her caring for her son (aka one of the toughest jobs in the world), binging Netflix with her beloved husband, or chasing after her puppy (who should technically be an adult dog by now).

Denise Daye

Made in the USA
Las Vegas, NV
19 September 2022

55578557R00187